The Heroes of Maple

Jeff Landry

This is a work of fiction.

While the stalwart heroes of this story may share common
nomenclature with certain individuals, the characters are a
product of the author's imagination. Any resemblance to actual
persons, living or dead, is purely coincidental.

ISBN: 1976503779
ISBN-13: 978-1976503771

DEDICATION

To the Maple Room,
may you enjoy a lifetime of reading adventures.

CONTENTS

ACKNOWLEDGMENTS

This book would not exist were it not for the students and teachers of the Hill View Montessori Maple Room. They welcomed me into their classroom, shared their ideas, and gave me a reason to tell this story. So thank you, Helen Murphy, Cheryl Hood, and the students: Addison, Ariana, Eduardo, Izzy, Jackson, Jaydan, Jazylin, Johannah, Katelynn, Landen, Leo, Madi, Madison, Max, Michael, Myah, Owen, Pat, Stalin, Tyler, and of course, my daughter, Violet. And thank you to the entire Montessori Community for their support.

This book is coherent and readable because of the incredible efforts of my editors. Emily Bridges is an actual editing superhero, and my wife, Nikki, provided insightful, honest, and vital assistance early on. Thanks, as well, to Rachel Hodge, for her efforts.

1 THE QUEEN OF GRACE AND COURTESY

At long last, the realm of Maple was at peace.

And it was all thanks to Helen, Queen of Grace and Courtesy.

*   *   *

In the old days, the rulers of Maple were harsh and strict, passing down laws and judgement from high atop the towers of their castle. They cared little for the needs of their people. They ordered and the people followed. Those who didn't comply were punished. That was the way of things. The *only* way.

Then Helen arrived. She flew in on a rainbow, perched upon Jaydan, a snowy-white Pegasus with wings as bright as the sun. She soared through the dull gray sky trailing stardust in her wake. She wore an elaborate patchwork cloak of tattered and colorful fabric interwoven with pieces of scribbled-on paper. Written amongst the folds and layers of her fabulous cloak were curious math equations, quotations from famous books, images of plants and planets, and scientific doodles of everything from ants to atoms.

The cloak shimmered. The writing and drawings whirled and changed constantly as if caught in a storm. It was a cloak of powerful magic.

From atop her mighty Pegasus, Helen surveyed the land and saw great sadness. And she knew she must help.

So she travelled the land of Maple and talked to its people. She talked to the villagers, the farmers, and the builders. She talked with the pixies, the dwarves, and the trolls. She went to the sea and met with the merfolk; then she soared into the sky to speak with the birds.

But Helen was wise. She did more than talk. In fact, she didn't talk much at all. What she did was far more important.

She listened.

She listened to the people, the fairy-folk, and the animals of the land. She listened to their problems. She listened to their ideas.

And Helen came up with a plan.

* * *

The old rulers sat around a very long table dressed in gray suits and gray ties, their gray faces topped with gray hair. Their small eyes stared, unblinking, as an even smaller, grayer man pointed a thin stick at a gray chalkboard.

"Conformity," he wheezed through gray teeth, "is down." He pointed to a down-sloping line on the chalkboard. "This is unacceptable, gentlemen."

The dour gray gentlemen grumbled agreement.

"We must push harder," the small gray man demanded. "People are trying to 'be themselves,'" he said sourly. "We cannot have that."

He turned and pointed his long stick at one particular gray gentleman who had fashioned a small gray flower to his lapel.

"You," he seethed, "are you shouting enough?"

"Yes, sir!" was the automatic response.

"Then shout more," shouted the small gray man. "Never enough shouting, I say. And make more rules. The people love rules. They love being told what to do."

"Yes, sir!" was the automatic reply.

"Good. Very good," he wheezed. "Now, about this . . ."

CRASH!

The old gray man never finished his thought. Finishing thoughts is hard to do when your ceiling has suddenly crumbled in and your very long table has been replaced with a pile of rubble and a fabulous winged Pegasus.

"I'm sorry for the interruption," called Helen as she gracefully dropped from the back of the Pegasus. Her colorful cloak was a brilliant prism amongst the sea of dreary gray. "And sorry about the ceiling. We were aiming for the front door," she said with a wry look at her steed.

"*You* were aiming for the front door," said Jaydan the Pegasus. "I landed right where I wanted."

The old man sputtered. "It . . . it talks!"

"All the animals in Maple talk," said Helen calmly. "Did you not know that? No, you didn't. In fact, there are a great many things you do not know. But today, gentlemen, is your lucky day. Because I'm here to teach you."

And teach she did. Helen explained how the land of Maple should be ruled. The people would be free, she said, to find their own way. No more being told what to do. A ruler's job, she explained, was to provide a prepared environment for the people and give them the tools they need to succeed.

"Everyone is different," she proclaimed. "What's right for rock trolls may not be what's right for the pixies. You must adapt your tired old practices and guide each person in the way that will help them best. By doing so, you will create a better world."

The gray men shook their gray heads with vigor. "No!" they shouted. "Our way is the only way! People must conform. We have rules! Legislation has been passed! *Legislation!*"

Jaydan the Pegasus blew a long, loud raspberry. The gray men sputtered in horror.

"I don't even know what half of those words mean," said Jaydan, "and I can tell they're nothing but noise."

"Jaydan, that's impolite," chided Helen. Then she turned her attention to the gray men and smiled. "Your people are unhappy: fighting, arguing, and mad. They must learn to build bridges, not burn them. You must create a world that encourages independence, freedom within limits and a sense of order. Grant your people individual choice and let them figure out the best way to use and protect their environment."

The gray men did not understand the curious woman's innovative ideas. So they did what they did best.

They ordered.

They directed.

They shouted.

Oh, did they shout.

"You are but one woman!" they shouted.

"And a Pegasus," said Jaydan wryly. "Don't forget me. I'm pretty awesome."

The gray men scowled. "You are but one woman, and a rude flying horse!" they shouted. "You cannot stop us!"

Helen smiled.

"One woman can make a world of difference," she replied. "You would do well to remember that. But today, I am not alone."

Helen whistled.

And their gray palace exploded in color.

In rushed knights in gleaming armor. In stormed trolls, massive and solid as boulders. In bounded dwarves, tripping over their long beards and tumbling in every direction. In flew pixies and fairies riding butterflies and birds, fluttering and tittering in high-pitched voices. In stomped elephants and lions and, somehow, a bear-sized snail being ridden by an elf.

In, too, walked the quiet scholars, hidden behind high stacks of dusty books. In came peacocks riding camels, and camels riding peacocks. Then there were monkeys and tigers and hedgehogs and salamanders, and lastly a unicorn with a rainbow mane who gave the Pegasus a wide smile.

They all rushed in together and stopped and looked at the sad, small, gray men as Helen spoke.

"You see, sirs, I am not alone."

So from that day on, Queen Helen ruled.

And she brought peace back to Maple.

Libraries were built. Schools, too. Scientists returned to their labs and began to uncover the secrets of the universe. Engineers built elaborate machines and artists created things amazing and wondrous. People learned how to get along, to work together, to work towards being peacemakers instead of troublemakers.

After a time, the gray men retreated into the shadows and eventually vanished. Everyone was happy. And all was well.

That is, until a dragon flew out of the sky and kidnapped the Queen!

2 HEROES UNITE

Lady Cheryl, Royal Advisor to the Queen of Grace and Courtesy, sat uncomfortably on the edge of the royal throne. She was surrounded by a glittering ring of five knights who stood looking sad and embarrassed.

Behind the throne lay Jaydan, looking even sadder. Queen Helen, her oldest friend, was gone.

"The royal guard fought bravely," said Lady Cheryl to the gathered crowd. "But the dragon was too powerful. And as you can see, quite large." She gestured to the gaping hole in the throne room wall, through which could be seen the first signs of the rising sun. The pinks and yellows of the morning sky were a cheerful contrast to the gloomy mood in the castle.

Lady Cheryl continued, "The dragon flew in last night, carrying with it a horde of goblins. They overwhelmed the guard, grabbed our beloved Queen Helen, and flew off into the night."

Many in the crowd sighed and shuffled their feet. Some cried. The pixies hovered somberly, their pixie dust lacking its normal sparkle.

Even Max, the massive rock troll, was emotional. He grabbed a nearby piece of cloth and blew his rocky nose into it . . .

. . . then promptly apologized to the poor dwarf who was still wearing the cloth as a shirt.

"Oops, sorry."

"It's OK, mate."

The Royal Advisor, though, was overcome with a feeling of warmth. Despite the sadness and the tragedy they had suffered, no one cursed the goblins. No one shouted the dragon's name in anger. No one threatened violence or revenge. There was no hate in the hearts of the people of Maple. The Queen had taught her subjects well, and that filled Lady Cheryl with pride.

For the people of Maple knew that the goblins were no different than anyone else. Yes, they had done a terrible thing in helping the dragon kidnap the Queen. But to most of the people of Maple, the goblins and the dragon were simply friends who didn't realize they were friends yet.

With sudden determination, the Captain of the Palace Guard, Izzy, turned and knelt before the throne. Voice wavering, she said, "On behalf of my fellow guards, I apologize for our failure and I ask for a chance to bring back the Queen."

The other guards nodded vigorously, their shiny metal armor clinking and clanking loudly as their heads bobbed.

Lady Cheryl smiled. "You did not fail, Captain Izzy. You've merely been given a new challenge to overcome. But I am afraid I cannot honor your request."

Izzy looked stricken, her shoulders slumped.

"But, Lady Cheryl . . ."

The Royal Advisor held up her finger and winked. "Come, now. You're palace guards. The palace guards can't go dashing around the realm, can they? Palace guards guard the palace, do they not?"

The guards nodded again, this time with less vigor and far less armor-clanking.

"That's why," said Cheryl, "I've decided that you're all fired as palace guards . . ."

Each guard reacted differently. Izzy's face sagged. Michael cried. Jackson began chewing his lip. Owen began to argue. Pat crouched down behind his massively oversized shield and hoped not to be noticed.

Lady Cheryl laughed. "You didn't let me finish. I'm firing you as palace guards – and naming you the very first ever Knights of Peace. Your first task will be to rescue our Queen!"

The entire room, including the newly-named knights, began to cheer. Cheryl unfurled a scroll and began to read.

"By royal proclamation, I hereby name Captain Izzy, Sir Michael, Sir Jackson, Sir Owen and Sir Pat as the first members of the Royal Knights of Peace! Their solemn duty is to spread peace throughout the land of Maple and beyond. They will show care and consideration for the environment and for all creatures great or small. They will act with courtesy, grace, and respect. They will resolve conflicts with empathy and understanding. Their motto: never cruel, always kind."

The crowd cheered with excitement and glee. Animals roared joyously. Pixie dust showered the room. The dwarf tried to high-five the rock troll but was too short and missed, whacking his hand on the giant troll's stony knee.

"Ouch."

"Sorry," said Max.

Izzy silenced the crowd with a raised hand and pronounced boldly, "As the Knights of Peace, we will act with kindness. So we no longer need these trappings of war! We won't need these shields!"

She dropped her shield to the stone floor. It clanked very, very loudly.

"I mean . . ." said Michael hesitantly.

"And we don't need this armor, for we are Knights of Peace," Izzy announced.

She unstrapped her armor and let it fall to her feet. As you'd imagine — lots of clanking.

"Are you sure you've thought this through?" asked Jackson nervously.

Sir Pat again crouched down behind his massively oversized shield and hoped not to be noticed.

"And these swords," Captain Izzy proclaimed, holding her sword high in the air, "will only weigh us down as we combat the dragon with love and understanding!"

Before she could throw her sword away, Sir Owen gently grabbed her arm and said calmly, "We should probably keep the swords."

"Keep the swords?"

All four knights nodded vigorously in response. More clanking. So much clanking.

"Love and understanding sounds like a great plan, but we're not so sure the dragon will agree right away," reasoned Owen. "Might take some convincing."

"Huh, OK, if you think it's best," conceded Izzy.

"And you know," said Jackson, "the armor is rather stylish. It makes us look pretty cool."

"And shiny," added Michael.

"I can see my reflection in your butt," said Owen as he pulled out a comb and fixed his hair.

Pat, from behind his shield, called, "And the shields are great for sledding should we come upon any snowy hills."

"I do like sledding," said Izzy.

"Me too," grumbled Max the rock troll. Everyone looked at him, surprised. "What?" he asked. "Sledding is fun."

The dwarf tittered. "When you go sledding, is it like . . . a rock slide?!"

The crowd laughed heartily at the pun while the Royal Advisor rolled her eyes. She tried to get everyone back on track.

"Keep your swords and shields and armor, yes. Hopefully, you will not need them. For the Knights of Peace must always try to solve problems with logic, reason, and understanding."

Again, the room erupted in cheers. But from beneath the rumble of noise came a small voice.

The small voice came from a small person – or, more accurately, a small otter – standing in the back of the room. The otter wore thick glasses and wore a pink bow tie because, as she had often heard, bow ties are cool.

"I'd like to help," said the otter, whose name was Katelynn. "Though I'm not sure if I would be much help. I'm *just* a librarian, after all."

"Just!" came a shout. "Just?!! Librarians are the guardians of knowledge and wisdom. Of *course* you'd be helpful."

The crowd parted to reveal Johannah the unicorn, her rainbow mane and tail glimmering in the morning light. She strode purposefully towards the otter and put a gentle hoof on her shoulder.

"You will be a great help. And I will, too. If there's something to be done to get our Queen back, count me in."

At this, Jaydan the Pegasus finally stirred. She rose and stretched her wide, bright wings.

"It looks like we're forming a rescue party," she said. "Helen is my oldest friend. I will do anything to save her."

Others stepped forward, too.

Everyone, in fact.

The entire realm wanted to help.

After much discussion, the rock troll, Max, was chosen to go. Madison the elf and her bear-sized snail, Stripey, were also picked. The pixies volunteered their bravest, who was also named Madison, to join the rescue party.

"We can't have two Madisons in one story!" shouted Owen. "That's confusing!"

"All my friends call me Madi," offered the pixie.

"Madi is a good name for a pixie," said Jaydan wisely.

"Madi the pixie, Madison the elf," said Michael. "I think I can keep that straight."

"You are all brave, Heroes of Maple!" proclaimed the Royal Advisor. "Go forth and find the Queen of Grace and Courtesy! Bring her home safely! Go! Go! Go!"

The cheers were deafening. The room shook from the sound. For five minutes the people cheered. Ten minutes. Twenty. Finally, the heroes gathered together and marched for the door, hugging and high-fiving as they went. They poured out of the throne room, marched through the castle halls and down into the expansive courtyard with great purpose.

And then, again, the small voice of the otter broke through the chaos.

"Er, um, anyone know which way we're going?"

And in fact, no one did.

3 THE ASTRONOMER'S TOWER

The courtyard was quiet. The Royal Advisor had sent the crowd home, leaving the heroes to come up with a plan.

Above them loomed the majestic Maple Castle. Half stone castle, half gigantic maple tree, it was a sight that inspired wonder and awe.

The Knights of Peace stood in a loose cluster with Jaydan the Pegasus; Johannah the unicorn; the rock troll, Max; the pixie, Madi; and Katelynn the otter. Madison the elf was circling the group on her snail, leaving a trail of slippery goo in their wake.

"So," said Jaydan sourly, "no one knows where the dragon lives?"

"Until today, we didn't even know we *had* a dragon," confessed Sir Jackson glumly.

Johannah stomped a hoof in frustration. "Well, didn't any of you see which way the dragon flew off?"

Sir Owen shook his head. "It was dark. And I had goblin drool in my eyes."

"We got hit with the dragon's tail," said Izzy, gesturing to herself and Jackson. "We were upside-down and didn't see him fly off."

Head lowered, Sir Michael offered, "A goblin turned my helmet around and was whacking me in the butt with my own sword."

Everyone groaned in sympathy.

The group then turned to Pat, who was crouched down and hiding behind his massively oversized shield.

"I was doing this," he said meekly from behind the shield.

"Well," said Madi, "someone must have seen something!"

"But who would have been out that late looking at . . . the . . . sky . . ." said Katelynn, trailing off as she raised her eyes up . . .

. . . and up . . .

. . . and up . . .

. . . until she saw what she was looking for. She was craning her neck back so far, she actually tipped over backwards.

"I know what to do," Katelynn said from the ground excitedly.

The rest of the group followed her gaze up, up, up to the tallest tower in the castle. At the top was a small observatory that housed a giant telescope.

The Astronomer's Tower.

"Yes, yes, yes!" squealed Izzy. "The night owl would surely have seen what happened! Knights of Peace, to me!"

With noisy clamor, the Knights of Peace formed an uneven line behind their captain.

"Knights," she called dramatically, "we have our path. We must scale the

Astronomer's Tower, the tallest in the land. The climb will be hard."

"I hear it has 10,000 steps," said Michael.

"No way, it's more like 100,000," said Owen.

"I heard it goes on forever and ever," said Pat from behind his shield.

"Guys," said Jaydan. In their fervor, they ignored her.

"It will try our bodies, my friends, but we will climb a million steps if need be," said Izzy with booming oration.

"Guys," said Jaydan again.

"No obstacle is too great to keep us from our Queen!"

The Knights raised their fists and roared in patriotic excitement.

"Excuse me," said Jaydan.

"Knights, to the Astronomer's Tower!"

With that, the five Knights of Peace were off at a run. Their armor clanked in a chaotic symphony of ear-splitting noise that drowned out the voices of their companions. Caught up in the excitement, Max bellowed a throaty growl (which sounded like two bricks smashing a tuba) and lumbered after them.

In moments, they were gone.

Stretching her wide wings, Jaydan rolled her eyes and looked knowingly at the otter.

"I have wings," she said, "Do you want me to just fly you up there?"

"Yes, please."

Katelynn climbed up onto Jaydan's broad back and they quickly took to the air.

"Wait for me!" called Madi, her tiny wings shedding sparkling pixie dust as she hurried after them.

"Humph," snorted Johannah as she watched them fly away. "Well, what are we supposed to do?"

From atop her snail, Madison produced a greasy square box. "Want some pizza?"

"Where did you get pizza?"

"I keep it in Stripey's shell," said Madison. "She's got loads of room in there."

Johannah made a face. "Ew, snail pizza? I think I'll just look around for goblins or something."

Madison shrugged and took a big bite. "Suit yourself!"

*   *   *

Jaydan, Katelynn, and Madi flew up to the Observatory. They landed on a short, rickety porch and knocked on a sturdy wooden door.

"Who," came a muffled call from behind door.

"It's the librarian, Katelynn, here with some friends. We need your help."

"Who," again said the voice behind door.

"My friends?" asked Katelynn, a little confused. "I'm with Jaydan the Pegasus and Madi the pixie."

"Who," was once again the reply.

"Look, it doesn't matter who we are. We need your help. Something terrible has happened."

The sturdy wooden door swung inwards, revealing Landen, a scowly little owl. He was wearing a pair of owl-sized jeans and a blue t-shirt printed with the words "owl you need is love."

The owl sized up the trio of visitors on his porch and hooted his displeasure.

"I wasn't asking *who* you were," he sniped. "I was telling you, in *Owl-speak*, to go away! I'm very busy doing my calculations. There's an asteroid, you know. It might even hit us!"

Landen seemed weirdly happy about that.

"Wouldn't that be bad?" asked Madi.

"Yes!" he replied with a goofy, giddy smile.

"I'm really sorry to bother you," said Katelynn, "but this is an emergency. We really need your help."

Landen the owl sighed. "Fine, fine. Come in, come in. But don't touch anything!"

The Observatory was a small room filled with tipsy stacks of books and rolls of star charts. In the center of the room was the giant telescope that extended far out through the room's open ceiling. There was a tidy-looking nest of twigs, branches, and moss built at the base of the telescope.

"Did you see anything last night?" asked Katelynn.

"Did I see anything?" hooted the owl with wide eyes. "My friend, I saw infinity. I saw the birth and death of a thousand thousand stars. I saw swirling nebula, dazzling pulsars, and icy comets streaking through the vastness of space. And, it was amazing!"

"Yeah, but did you see anything useful?" asked Jaydan curtly.

The owl's small beak dropped open in horror.

"Get out," he whispered menacingly.

"Wait! No, please! We need your help," begged Katelyn. "The Queen's been kidnapped."

"What Queen?" asked Landen.

"Our Queen! Helen, the Queen of Grace and Courtesy!" cried Katelynn.

"We have a Queen?"

The otter was too dumbstruck to answer. So the pixie replied for her.

"Yes," she said, "we have a Queen! You live in her castle, you know. She was taken by a dragon last night!"

"We have dragons?" asked Landen innocently.

"Apparently so," sniped Katelynn, taking off her glasses and rubbing the bridge of her little otter nose.

"Well you don't have to be so rude about it. Up until just now I didn't know we had talking otters, either. And frankly, they aren't all that pleasant. I do like your bow tie, though. Bow ties are cool."

"Please," begged Jaydan, trying to be the voice of reason, "you're up here all night long, and you can see far and wide. Did you see anything that might have looked like a dragon flying away from the castle?"

"Hmmm, OK," said Landen as he shuffled through a pile of papers, "let me see. Queen, you say? Blonde hair?"

"Yes, yes!" they shouted in reply.

"Fancy cloak, looks like somebody tried to hide a rainbow in a textbook?"

"Yes, yes, that's her! That's her!"

"Riding a dragon, you say?" asked Landen.

"Yes! Did you see them?"

"Nope, but I did find the invitation to her coronation from years ago," replied Landen, holding up a colorful invitation pulled from the pile of papers. "Looks like she was riding a Pegasus, not a dragon. Seems like you guys ought to get your story straight. Heh heh heh. Get it? *Otter* get your story straight? Because you're an otter. Oh my, I made a joke."

"Not helpful," squeaked Madi in frustration.

"Listen," reasoned Katelynn, "you've got this giant telescope here. I bet it can see far and wide, right?"

"It sees everything," said Landen proudly.

"Great! Perfect! How about you swing it around the realm of Maple and see if you can find a dragon?"

Landen turned his full attention to Katelynn and Jaydan. Madi, momentarily forgotten, fluttered around behind him and, without his notice, began peering into the eyepiece of the telescope.

"Well, that's unheard of. This is a finely tuned piece of machinery. Its purpose is to look deep into space. There is simply no way I could make this incredible technology work to find something as pedestrian as an earthbound object--"

"Found them," said Madi.

"What?" asked Katelynn.

"What?" asked Jaydan.

"Who!" hooted Landen, though he was speaking *Owl* and it wasn't a very nice word he said.

"Right there, see?" said Madi. "A dragon, flying around."

The little otter scurried over to the telescope, despite the owl's wing-flapping objection, and peered into the eyepiece. And there, indeed, was a dragon far off in the distance flying around the tip of a rocky mountain.

"Oh, that makes sense," said Katelynn.

"What?" asked the Pegasus.

"That's Dragon Mountain," Katelynn explained matter-of-factly. "It's in the mountains north of Maple."

"Wait," snapped Jaydan sharply, "we've got a 'Dragon Mountain' in Maple and it never occurred to you that the dragon might live there?"

"Not actually *in* Maple, but no, it didn't."

"It ought to have," said Landen, never one to miss the chance to make a pun. "Heh heh. Get it? It *otter* have! Oh, otter jokes are fun!" He clapped his wings happily.

"We have our destination. We need to go," said Jaydan urgently as Katelynn clumsily climbed onto the Pegasus's back. "We have a long journey ahead of us. Landen, thank you very much for your help. We're very sorry for the intrusion."

The owl waved his wing. "Happy to do my civic duty. It's important to care about the community, you know. But get out, get out. I really do need to figure out where this asteroid is going to hit." After a moment, the owl smiled. "You *otter* get out of here. Heh heh."

Madi waved as she fluttered out. Jaydan flew out with a mighty flap of her massive wings, sending a gust of wind throughout the room. Papers flew everywhere.

"Who!" shouted Landen in annoyance.

At the very same minute, the door on the other side of the room burst open. A clinking, clanking heap of red-faced, sweaty, and breathless knights stumbled through the door. A moment later, a rock troll fell on top of them.

"*Who*," moaned Landen as he rolled his eyes.

4 THE JOURNEY BEGINS

Now that they knew where to go, the Heroes of Maple gathered in the castle courtyard to discuss how they would get there.

In Maple, all roads lead north. The castle sits on a small island on the southern tip of the realm. Three wide bridges connect the castle to the mainland. Each bridge leads to a road. The Coastal Road runs along the Great Sea, the Mountain Road through the rocky eastern regions, and the Forest Road meanders north through the wooded mainland. All three roads

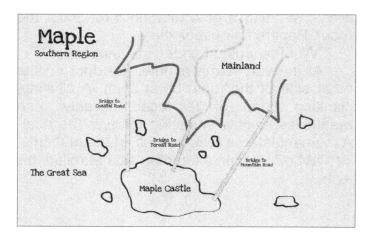

end up at the same spot – the base of Dragon Mountain.

The Heroes argued over which way to go. Katelynn grew frustrated at the group's inability to pick a road. She offered to run to her library to fetch a map so they could make an informed decision. The group agreed.

But Katelynn never returned.

Worried that she ran into trouble, Izzy and Michael went to find her. The others stayed behind and continued to debate.

*   *   *

"This adventure is not getting off to a good start," said Izzy as they walked quickly through the castle hallway. She was unhappy. She still felt guilty about what happened to the Queen.

"We'll be okay," said the ever-positive Michael. "Queen Helen has taught us patience. We are all very different. It will take time for us to learn how to work together."

"Yeah, but how much time?" she asked sadly.

They reached the door to the library, which was in one of the lower levels of the castle.

The library door was ajar. When Michael tried to push the heavy wooden door open farther, it wouldn't budge.

He looked at Izzy, suddenly worried. Something was very wrong.

Working together, the two knights heaved open the door. The library was a disaster.

Books were everywhere. Ripped pieces of paper were scattered all over. Shelves had been toppled.

The knights carefully walked into the clutter and began to look for Katelynn. After a few moments, they found her. She was cowering in a dark alcove in the far back of the library, clutching a book.

And she was not alone.

Two goblins, short and wiry with wild green-and-orange hair and stubby red horns and claws as long as pencils, were just a few feet away. They were so intent on upending a very old bookshelf, they didn't notice Katelynn or the knights.

With a crash, the bookshelf went down. The goblins howled with glee as they hopped and pointed at something that had been hidden for a very long time.

It was an iron ring attached to the floor.

Working quickly, the goblins grabbed the iron ring and pulled. A slab of stone came up from the floor.

The goblins had found a secret passageway!

Katelynn's eyes were wide. Bad enough they had trashed her library, but for them to know about a secret passage that she'd only heard whispers about – that was too much.

"Hey!" she shouted angrily at the goblins.

As soon as they spun around and set their small, golden eyes on her, she realized her mistake.

"Oh, dear," she whispered.

The goblins then noticed the knights and hissed. Whether the hissing was in anger or fear wasn't clear.

It was fear, however, that drove the knights into action. Michael drew his sword, only to drop it because his hands were shaking so much.

Izzy forgot she even had a sword and opted to run headlong at the goblins. She grabbed one of them and began wrestling him to the ground. But the goblin was strong, and soon the two were in a tangle, rolling around the floor.

Michael looked warily at the other goblin. Raising a hand, the knight said softly, "Let's just calm down, okay?"

The goblin was holding something – an orb of some kind. It was a deep, deep black but also somehow glowing. An item of magic, no doubt, and powerful.

"Please," said Michael. "Whatever it is, don't do it."

He took a step forward, but stopped when Izzy and her goblin rolled past, shouting and tugging and hair-pulling. They rolled back and forth, forward and backward, until they ended up right at the edge of the hole in the floor.

And then they fell in.

"No!" shouted Michael. He scurried over and peered down into the passageway. He saw nothing but darkness and heard not a sound.

To his left, the goblin with the orb suddenly made a run for the library exit.

Michael panicked. He didn't know what to do. Chase the goblin, or follow Izzy? He cast a quick look at Katelynn, but before she could say anything, he leapt into the dark hole and was gone.

"Oh, come on!" shouted Katelynn, her voice echoing around the trashed library.

She was alone.

Sighing heavily, the little otter took the book she had been clutching to her chest and tossed it down the dark passage. The knights would need it.

She then ran for the door. She knew what the other goblin had in his hand, and she had to stop him.

*   *   *

Jaydan was frustrated. Three members of their group had gone off, and those remaining couldn't agree on anything.

She understood their fear. Queen Helen had been an important part of all of their lives. Her absence weighed like a heavy blanket on their hearts. They were all upset and acting on edge.

Except for the elf, that is. Madison was pretty chill about everything.

But for the others, their fear was driving them beyond reason. They argued about everything, from the road to take, to what supplies to bring, to who should walk in the front and who should bring up the rear.

Jaydan didn't know what to do about it.

Some heroes, she thought bitterly.

When a goblin scurried into the courtyard clutching a curious black orb, all the arguing stopped.

"Stop him!" came a haggard cry. It was Katelynn, stumbling awkwardly into the courtyard. She was out of breath from running. "We . . . can't . . . let him . . ."

The Heroes began to surround the goblin, whose eyes darted this way and that, looking for an escape. With three knights, a rock troll, a unicorn, a Pegasus, a pixie, and a snail-riding elf surrounding him, there was nowhere to go.

The goblin shouted something (it may have been "sorry") and raised his hand in the air . . .

"No!" cried Katelynn.

. . . and smashed the black orb to the ground.

For a second, nothing happened, and the goblin looked a mix of relieved and confused.

Then the world crackled.

Static electricity filled the air, setting hairs standing on end.

Light blossomed in an explosion, and the very fabric of space and time ripped open. A shockwave sent the heroes flying to the ground. When they were able to get up, they saw it. There, in the middle of the courtyard, was a spinning, burning, bright hole in the air.

And goblins were pouring out of it.

Snarling and shouting, the goblins came. Clutching heavy clubs, they ran willy-nilly throughout the courtyard. They yelled and hopped and smashed and chased. They were chaos brought to life.

After a time, the hole closed with a pop.

The heroes did their best to contain the goblins but there were too many. There was nothing the heroes could do.

But all was not lost.

For the castle still housed someone who had no fear of a chaotic horde of unruly goblins. Not even a thousand thousand goblins would have challenged her.

For there at the castle door was Lady Cheryl, Royal Advisor to the Queen of Grace and Courtesy.

She strode calmly and quietly into the swirling hurricane of goblins, her shawl flapping, and raised her arms over her head. With one motion, she clapped.

The clap boomed.

"Heroes of Maple," she called, her voice carrying throughout the courtyard, "Go! Take the roads north and find the Queen! I'll deal with this lot!"

The goblin mass was still churning throughout the yard, so the heroes could not gather together. They could only rush to the gates closest to them.

Owen grabbed a trembling Pat by the collar and pulled him towards the coastal road.

Madison trailed behind them, urging her snail along gently.

Jackson sprinted for the forest road, little Madi clutching his collar and Katelynn tucked under his arm. A cluster of goblins began to follow them.

Jaydan took to the air and flew towards the mountain road, Johannah galloping and Max lumbering along with her.

As Jaydan flew away, she could hear the commanding voice of Lady Cheryl boom, "Goblins! That. Is. Enough!"

The castle was in good hands.

5 FROM DARKNESS TO FIRE

Izzy was sore.

The fall down the hole had not been pleasant.

Having a goblin clinging to her didn't help. He screamed and spit and bit most of the way down. Her armor offered some protection, but she was still scratched from the goblin's sharp claws.

And that fall. It went on for a long, long time.

At some point she was able to dislodge the goblin, so when she eventually hit bottom she did so on her own. She heard the goblin *oomph* down next to her, then scurry away.

She couldn't see him, though. It was pitch black.

A few seconds later, Michael plowed into her, causing a whole new set of problems.

"Nice rescue," she said, pushing him off with a grunt. "What happened to the other goblin?"

Michael did not answer.

"Oh, come on, really? You let him get away so you could come after me?"

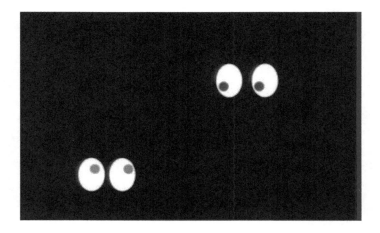

She sounded mad, but also a little touched.

"Sorry," muttered Michael.

"If I could see you, I'd hug you. Kick you, too, but I'd start with a hug."

"Ow," said Michael.

"What? I didn't actually kick you."

"Something just hit me," he said, nervous. She could hear him shuffling around in the dark. "It's a book. Did Katelynn throw a book in after us?"

"I bet it's important," answered Izzy. "She must have figured out what the goblins were looking for."

"What do you think is down here?"

"I have no idea. My guy ran off," she said. "Goblins must see better in the dark."

"Wonderful news!" said Michael with a laugh. "So what do we do?"

Izzy shrugged, then laughed because Michael couldn't see her in the dark. "Well, we fell so far, I don't think we can get back up the way we came. I guess we'll just have to feel around and hope we find something useful."

For fifteen minutes they slowly felt around in the darkness, growing frustrated and more than a little scared. Finally, Michael's right hand found something unusual on the wall. It was a small bump, too round and smooth to be natural.

"I think I found something," he said softly. "It's some kind of button."

"So push it," she said. "What's the worst that could happen?"

"It could drop snakes on us," he said.

"It could drop pies," she replied hopefully.

"Or, maybe a pie full of snakes," Michael said with a laugh.

"I could eat," smiled Izzy.

Michael got serious. "OK, I'm going to push it. You ready?"

"Ready."

He pushed it.

There were no snakes. No pies, either. There was, however, light.

Just not much. A small panel to his left lit up with an eerie, dull green glow.

"Magic," he muttered. He felt Izzy step up behind him.

"What does it mean?" she asked.

The glowing panel had two words engraved onto its surface – the word "dark" was written above the word "fire."

Between the two words were two rows of four dashes. It looked like:

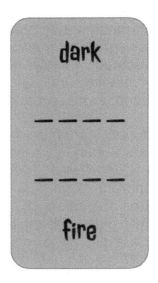

"Hey, look at this," said Michael. A small piece of chalk was hanging next to the panel on a piece of silver chain.

"It looks like a word ladder," said Izzy. "Maybe we have to complete it."

"OK, fine, so how do we do that?"

"Don't you remember word ladders?" she asked. "All you need to do is change one letter in each word until you get to the new word."

Michael nodded. "I remember now. Okay, I get it. So, how do we turn darkness into fire?"

The two thought for a moment.

"I got it!" shouted Izzy with excitement. She grabbed the piece of chalk. "What if we change the 'k' in 'dark' to an 'e' to make 'dare?'"

"Yeah," said Michael. "Then we can change the 'a' to an 'i' to make the word 'dire' – which is what our situation looks like right now."

"Then we make 'dire' into 'fire' by replacing the 'd' with an 'f,'" she finished. With neat handwriting, she completed the word ladder.

As soon as she finished writing the words, the cavern lit up with fire. Torches, bracketed to the wall but unseen in the dark, came to life. Izzy and Michael had to shield their eyes from the sudden brightness.

Once they could see, the knights whistled in awe. They were in a rough stone cavern. To the right of the panel was a hallway that seemed to stretch on forever.

"Guess we're going that way," said Izzy.

Michael looked at the book that Katelynn had thrown down after them.

"Huh," he said, showing Izzy the title, "*Secrets of the Dragon's Treasure*." He flipped through the pages quickly, stopping when he came to a page that said "from darkness to fire" at the top.

"Well, this should be helpful," he said. "Katelynn definitely figured out what the goblins were looking for."

"I love that little librarian," said Izzy. "Come on, we've got a goblin to find."

"And apparently a treasure," said Michael. "Don't forget about the treasure."

"How could I?" she laughed, and the two knights started down the long hall together.

6 THE SQUIRREL-TOWN COUNT

Jackson ran.

Since he, Katelynn, and Madi had escaped the castle to the Forest Road, they had heard the howls and yelps of pursuing goblins. Madi had flown back to see how many were on their tail.

The greens, yellows, and oranges of autumn trees blurred past, but his eyes focused only on the road ahead. Any wayward root or hole could send him and his cargo tumbling.

Katelynn the otter was still tucked under his arm, and she was not happy.

"Ow, ow, ouch!" she whined loudly. "Why does armor have to feel so hard?"

"It's meant to stop swords," said Jackson tightly.

"Well, when was the last time someone tried to hit you with a sword?" she asked pointedly.

Actually, never, thought the knight, but he kept that to himself.

"Well, a couple hundred goblins just tried to smash my head in," he replied finally.

Katelynn humphed a quiet hmph. "I don't know that any of them *actually* tried to hit anyone," she said carefully. In fact, she thought it seemed like the swarming goblins were going out of their way to *not* hit anyone.

Jackson failed to appreciate the distinction. "What was that thing, anyway? That orb?"

"I'm not sure," replied Katelynn slowly. "I have an idea, though. Many years ago – shortly after the Queen arrived, an item went missing from my library."

"Let me guess," said the knight, "a creepy black orby thing that poops goblins."

Katelynn rolled her eyes. "Not exactly. It's a portal device. It opens doorways from one place to another. The dragon must have had a goblin army waiting back at Dragon Mountain. Those two in the library probably stayed behind after the Queen was kidnapped."

"Wonderful. Do you think they're still following us?" asked Jackson, risking a glance back over his shoulder.

When he turned back around, he ran headlong into a pixie.

"Oi!" shouted Madi, pixie dust spiraling as she did a mid-air tumble. "Watch your face, metal-man! And yes, they are following you, but they're moving much slower so you can take a break."

Glad for the respite, Jackson immediately dropped Katelynn to the ground and bent over onto his knees, gulping for air.

"Oh, don't worry about me," said Katelynn, brushing herself off. "Otters bounce."

Madi chuckled. Her wings were a blur, buzzing like a hummingbird. Her purple, star-speckled hair was wind-blown, but her eyes were bright with excitement.

"There are five following us," she said. "Looks like they're the only ones who left the castle. They don't seem all that interested in catching us, though. Mostly I think they were glad to be away from Cheryl."

Katelynn grinned. "She'll have them mopping floors and harvesting crops by nightfall, and happy to do it, too."

"Five is too many," said Jackson seriously. "I can't fight that many."

"You heard Cheryl," scolded Madi. "We aren't out here to fight."

Jackson flapped his arms in frustration. "Well I'm not just going to let a bunch of goblins eat me!"

"I think goblins are vegetarians," said Katelynn quietly, almost to herself. "I think I read that somewhere. Oh, I wish I had my books."

"Yeah," said Jackson, "something else to carry."

"Oh, shush," said Madi, giving the knight a tap on the nose. The resulting splatter of pixie dust made him start to sneeze.

"Aaaaaaaa-*chooooooooo!*"

"Oops, sorry about that, Sir Jackson."

"Don't worry about it – it – it-*chooooooo!*"

"Come on," said Katelynn. "Let's keep moving. We need to stay ahead of those goblins."

They walked for a while. Katelynn's short otter legs and Jackson's heavy armor made for a slow pace, but Madi's backtracking confirmed the goblins were moving equally slow.

"Maybe they're getting tired," she guessed.

"Maybe they don't want to catch us," offered Katelynn softly.

The winding forest road soon came to a small clearing. Massive oak trees loomed in a rough circle. Little doors and windows, patios and porches dotted the trunks and branches of the towering trees. In the center of the clearing was a giant pile of acorns.

"Ooo, Squirrel-town," squeaked Madi. "I love Squirrel-town! It's so cozy!"

At the sound of her voice, dozens of little squirrel heads popped out of doors and windows. They all chirped and chattered happily.

"Madi!" called one small red squirrel.

"Jazylin!" replied Madi. She swooped down and gave the squirrel a pixie-dust-filled hug.

Madi then introduced the squirrel to her companions as the mayor of Squirrel-town. After polite introductions, Jackson got serious.

"There are goblins coming down the road after us. You aren't safe."

Jazylin looked stricken. She gestured to the pile of acorns. "It's harvest time. We need to count and store these acorns before winter comes. We can't leave them out here for a bunch of goblins to eat!"

Jackson assessed the pile. He sighed. "There is no way we can count all of these acorns in time. There must be thousands of them. It would take days."

"Well," said Jazylin, "I guess you better go fight some goblins, then." The squirrel crossed her arms stubbornly and glared at the knight.

Katelynn raised her hand shyly. "I, um, I have an idea."

Jackson drew his sword and held it out to the little otter. "You want to fight them?" he asked.

The little otter flailed her arms at the sword. "Ew, no, get it away, get it away!" Composing herself, she continued, "No, I have a way to count the acorns quickly. But it will require a little pixie magic."

Madi spun in a tight, flourishing circle. "I've got all the magic you need, little friend!"

Katelynn picked up an acorn. "You might remember the Queen teaching this to us. Think of this acorn as a unit."

She placed it on the ground, and then grabbed nine more acorns and lined them up in a row.

"That," she said, "is a ten bar. Ten acorns in a row. Now, Madi, can you pixie-magic me nine more rows of ten acorns right here?"

Madi twinkled her feet and waved her arms. Acorns began to float through the air. After much *ooh*ing and *aah*ing from the onlooking squirrels, there were ten rows of ten acorns together on the ground.

"That," said Katelynn, "is a square. Ten rows of ten, which is how many acorns, Jazylin?"

The red squirrel scrunched her face up as she did the math in her head. "One hundred?"

Katelynn clapped. "Yes, one hundred acorns in a square. Now, Madi, if you would, can you stack nine more squares on top of this one?"

More pixie dust, more *ooh*ing and *aah*ing, and finally there was a cube of acorns ten across, ten high, and ten deep.

"That's a thousand acorns!" shouted Jazylin excitedly. "That's amazing!" She beckoned to a few squirrels. "Get that up into the trees where the goblins can't find it," she ordered.

With the cube held together with Madi's magic, the squirrels had no trouble getting it to safety. While they worked, the pixie used her magic to sort out the rest of the acorns, ending up with a total of five full cubes.

"Wow, five thousand acorns," whistled Jazylin. "We are going to eat well this winter, aren't we, gang?"

"Acorn pie!" shouted a young squirrel.

"Acorn pizza!" came another shout.

Jackson, who had been watching the road for goblins, rushed back into the clearing.

"The goblins are coming! You've got to hide and we've got to run!"

Jazylin leapt into Katelynn's arms and gave the otter a hug.

"Thank you so much for helping us," she said. "You've saved our winter harvest. Go, run. We'll see if we can slow down those goblins as best as we can."

The knight grabbed Katelynn and once again tucked her under his arm (much to her dismay) and began to run for the northern stretch of the forest road.

"Thanks!" he called over his shoulder, but with all the clanking armor, no one but Katelynn heard him.

Madi lingered a moment. "Are you sure you're good?" she asked.

Jazylin grinned and nodded. "Oh, we'll be alright. Archers, to arms!"

Up popped three dozen squirrels, each holding a mini slingshot and a basket of pebbles.

Madi grinned and buzzed away. The sound of yelping goblins soon followed in her wake.

7 THE SEASHELL KNIGHT

The Coastal Road was the prettiest road in Maple. On one side was the vast blue sea, crashing against the white sandy beach. On the other side was an area of grassy dunes and short scrub pines filled with the hooting, cawing, chirping sounds of nature.

"This is amazing," smiled Owen.

"You said it," said Madison, lounging atop her snail, Stripey. "Beach life is the only way to live."

"How can you be so happy?" said Pat sadly. "Our Queen is missing and our castle is full of goblins!"

"Don't be such a downer," said Owen, punching Pat on the shoulder. "Lady Cheryl has the goblins under control."

"Besides," said Madison, "You aren't going to fix anything by being negative. Chin up – the view is better that way."

The snail smiled and bobbed his eyestalks happily.

"I found Stripey near the beach," remembered Madison. "I was just a tiny elfling, and I saw this beautiful shell on the side of the road. I thought it was empty, so I tossed it in my pocket. I put it on the kitchen table with the rest of my treasures. The next day, my not-so-empty shell crawled over to my plate and started eating my breakfast!"

Stripey let loose the snail version of a laugh.

"Yuck," said Pat, making a sour face. "There must have been slime all over the table!"

Madison shrugged. Owen chuckled.

"Scared of a little slime, Pat?" teased Owen.

"Oh, be quiet," Pat scowled. He took a step away from Owen and stepped into Stripey's snail trail with a squish.

"Ew, ew, ew!" he shouted, hopping around on one foot. He swiped at his boot with his hand and then realized that slimy hands are far worse than slimy boots. Pretty soon he had fallen down into a bush.

"Like I said," said Owen, offering a helping hand, "it's just a little slime."

"Why don't you guys walk in front of Stripey," offered Madison with a casual wave. "You're harshing my chill."

After Pat got his hands and feet wiped clean of slime, the two knights marched a little ways ahead.

"I'm sorry you got stuck with me," said Pat sadly.

Owen was shocked. "Stuck with you? We're friends! Why would you say that?"

Sniffing, Pat replied, "You're always teasing me, making me feel bad. I know I'm not as brave as the rest of you. Do you really think I need to be reminded of that?"

"I thought —" started Owen, then stopped. He thought back to all the things he'd said to Pat in the past and tried to understand what his friend was feeling. He never meant to be mean. He just thought he was being funny. Feeling bad, he looked down at his feet . . .

. . . and saw something…

. . . but the world moved too fast for him to realize what it was before it was too late. There was a snap, a twang, and suddenly he and Pat were hanging upside-down from a tree. Their armor clinked and clanked against one another.

"*Wooo-hooo*! I got one!" said a voice from the trees. A moment later, the voice emerged.

His hair was stringy and braided with long pieces of slimy green seaweed, which stuck out from underneath a conch shell helmet. He wore a vest of scallop shells knitted together with wire. He had clam shells strapped to his shoulders, elbows, and knees.

His excitement turned to confusion when he saw two knights swinging from his trap.

"You're not goblins! Darn it, get down from there, you two! Stop messing with my traps!" His voice was stern but not unkind.

By now, Madison and Stripey had arrived on the scene. Still relaxed, the elf chuckled and said, "Oh, hey Stalin. I was wondering if I'd see you out here."

"Madison! Stripey! What a nice surprise!" called Stalin happily. "But you shouldn't be out here. Goblins are afoot."

With a nod, Madison replied, "That is exactly why we're here."

Stalin nodded and pointed up at Owen and Pat. "Who're the tin cans up there?"

"That's Owen and Pat. They're Knights of Peace. Guys, this is Stalin. He's known around these parts as the Seashell Knight."

"Nice to meet you," said Pat.

"Is it?" asked Owen.

Madison scowled at Owen but continued. "The Queen's been kidnapped by a dragon and a bunch of goblins. We're on our way to save her."

"Well, you can count on me. I'll help fight them," said Stalin.

From up above, Pat called, "We're not here to fight them. We're here to reason with them."

Rolling his wild eyes, Stalin asked, "Is he serious?"

Madison nodded gravely. "It's the Queen's way, man."

Stalin chewed on this for a moment and then shrugged. "Eh, I suppose it is her way. But goblins aren't always good for talking, you know."

Owen interrupted him. "Goblins!" he shouted and pointed, which caused him and Pat to start spinning around. "Whoa, whoa, I'm getting dizzy. On the . . . whoa . . . on the beach!"

There were three goblins, short and wiry and moving carefully along the beach. They were looking at something, but Owen couldn't make it out since he was still spinning around.

"Dizzy," moaned Pat.

"Yup, that'll be the cake," said Stalin.

"What cake?" asked Madison.

Owen could just make out what looked like a large chocolate cake sitting on the beach. It was clearly what the goblins were moving towards.

"I see it," he said. "What's it for?"

"I'm getting sick up here," said Pat woozily.

"Bait," said Stalin.

"Bait for what?" Madison asked urgently.

The goblins neared the cake. They were practically on top of it. One of them barked something inaudible, then reached out his club and nudged the cake.

There was another snap, another twang, and all three goblins were flipped up into the air and thrown into the ocean. Stalin had cleverly hidden a catapult under the sand.

"You booby-trapped the cake!" shouted Madison. "That's cruel."

"Not as cruel as being hung upside-down," whined Pat.

"Hey, guys," said Owen. "I don't think goblins can swim."

He was right. The goblins were flailing in the water, bobbing up and down and flapping their arms uselessly.

"We need to save them," said Madison.

She moved fast. Being an elf, she was gifted with great speed and reflexes. In one motion she leapt into the air, pulled Owen's sword from its sheath, and sliced through the rope that was holding the knights upside-down. By the time they crashed to the ground, Madison was already sprinting down the beach towards the water.

"Hey, I found something worse than hanging," said Pat. "Falling."

"Falling's fine," said Owen. "It's the crashing that's bad. Come on."

He pulled his friend up and the two knights began running towards the water.

Stalin sighed. "You can't go in the ocean with armor on, you fools! You'll sink! Oh, alright, I'll help, too," he said as he headed to the beach.

With heroic effort, Madison managed to pull the goblins out of the water and onto the beach. She then helped Stalin pull the well-intentioned knights, Owen and Pat, out of the ocean before they drowned.

"Told you that you can't go into the ocean in armor," Stalin chided. Both Owen and Pat looked away sheepishly.

"Thanks for pulling us out," said Pat softly.

Stalin waved him off. "My fault in the first place." At that, he turned to the goblins. They looked so small, curled up and breathing heavily on the beach. Small and harmless. "And you folk . . . I'm sorry, too. That was a cruel trick to play on someone."

The goblins did not know how to respond. They weren't used to having people apologize to them.

Owen stood up and pulled off his helmet – which caused a large amount of water to splash down onto his head. He looked at the goblins, then over at his friend Pat, and smiled.

"Seems like a lot of problems between people come from not understanding one another," he said. Then he reached out his hand. "Hi, my name's Owen. What's yours?"

8 MUSHROOM CAP LAB

After passing through a few friendly villages and warning them of what had happened at the castle, Jaydan, Max, and Johannah continued north. The Mountain Road cut through a mix of woodland and rocky terrain. A steep cliff wall stood along the side of the road.

One village, though, brought with it some dire news.

An army of goblins had been sighted farther north, not far past the Mushroom Cap Lab.

"What's the Mushroom Cap Lab?" Jaydan asked. Before long, she found out.

The lab was a curious sight. The building was constructed like a giant mushroom with a collection of smaller mushrooms built on top. Those smaller mushrooms had even smaller mushroom-shaped buildings on top of them, and so on, until the smallest rooms at the top of the lab were no bigger than a mouse. The mushroom-shaped roofs of each building were colorfully painted – no two colors were the same.

"Ooo, I love the colors," said Johannah. "And I thought scientists were boring."

Jaydan, gliding a few feet above, said, "Scientists are some of the most creative people I've ever met."

Max held up his stony hand and stopped short. "I hear something." He paused, then shook his head. "No. I feel something."

Jaydan heeded his warning and began circling in the sky, looking for trouble.

Johannah scoffed. "Oh, come on, Pebbles, you old worry-wart. Everything is fine. The goblins are still a few hours away."

Unworried, Johannah continued on to the lab. When she was only a couple of feet away, she raised a hoof to knock on the door. It was only then that she heard the building rumble.

"Uh-oh," she said before every door and window of the mushroom-shaped lab blew open and spilled forth bright orange foam. The warm, bubbly goo oozed out rapidly and piled on the ground like squeezed-out toothpaste.

Out of one of the upper windows came a joyful squeak. Riding down the foamy wave was a tiny mouse in a little white lab coat. She was balanced on a magnifying glass, riding down the ooze like she was on a surfboard.

"Wooooooo!" she shouted. "I'm catching some waves!"

The mouse came to a soft landing on the ground. She hopped off the magnifying glass, picked it up in her tiny mouse hands, and peered at the foamy residue.

"Whoa, look at those bubbles! Too much dish soap this time, I think. But feel that heat! Now that's an exothermic reaction!" It was only then that she noticed the foam-covered unicorn at her front door. "Oh, hi there. You're new. I'm Myah."

Johannah looked at Myah and said, "That . . . was . . . AWESOME!" With a horsey neigh, she began laughing and prancing around in the foamy goo. "It's like an outside bubble bath! How did you do this?"

A deep, gentle voice came from inside the lab. "We added activated yeast to a mixture of hydrogen peroxide, dish soap, and orange food coloring. As Myah said, a little too much dish soap. But overall, a successful test. Hi, I'm Tyler."

Through the front door came an elephant-shaped mass of orange foam. With a mighty trumpet of his trunk, the elephant-shaped foam blew himself clean and revealed there was, in fact, an elephant underneath.

"What do you call this?" asked Johannah as she pranced.

"Elephant's toothpaste," said Tyler as Myah squeaked "Mouse's toothpaste" at the same time. The two scientists glared at each other, then laughed.

"We're studying exothermic reactions," said Myah.

"Exo-whatsits?" asked Max, standing safely outside the foam line.

"Hey, you're made of rock," said Myah. "Cool!"

"Exothermic," explained Tyler. "That means it releases heat. Can you feel the heat coming off the foam?"

"I can," said Johannah. "And it feels Ah-MAY-zing!"

"It's a simple experiment," said Myah. "With the right ingredients, anyone can do it at home."

"Oh, I am totally doing this!" shouted Johannah.

"Not if we don't act fast, you aren't," called Jaydan from the air. "There are goblins ahead!"

"Goblins? What goblins?" asked Myah.

Quickly, Max and Johannah explained the situation to the scientists.

"We need to turn them back, or they'll destroy our lab," said Myah.

"But how?" asked Max.

"Let's think about this logically," said Tyler. "What do we know about goblins?"

"Well, they have poor eyesight," said Myah, "they are easily distracted. They love to smash stuff."

"Did you know they used to live in this valley?" asked Tyler. "It was many, many years ago."

"Why did they leave?" asked Johannah.

"They were driven out when the gray men were in charge," said Tyler. "That's how they ended up in the mountains. It's too bad. Goblins are talented storytellers."

Tyler pointed to a craggy peak that loomed over the road. "See that peak right there? There's an old goblin bedtime story that says the peak would turn into a volcano and erupt if the little goblin children misbehaved."

"Nice story," said Max dourly.

"Even though they left the valley long ago, that story has stuck with them and survived throughout the generations."

"It's not really a volcano, though, is it?" asked Johannah nervously.

Myah squeaked and shook her head. "No. But . . ."

The elephant's eyes went wide. "Myah, are you thinking what I'm thinking?"

"I sure am, Tyler," she replied giddily.

The others were confused. "What, what is it?" asked Max.

Tyler smiled. "It may not actually be a volcano, but we're going to turn it into one."

"Isn't that dangerous?" asked Johannah.

"Nope," said Myah. "It's awesome!"

*   *   *

Getting supplies out of a lab filled with bubbly orange foam was not easy. But they worked together and soon had everything at the top of the peak.

They had a bucket of baking soda, a large drum of vinegar, a giant bottle of red food coloring, and a bottle of dish soap.

"Ok," said Jaydan, hovering in the air and keeping a watchful eye out for goblins, "what do we do?"

"We need a hole – a big one," squeaked Myah.

Silently, Max raised a giant fist and punched down once, twice, three times. He easily made a crater big enough to fit an elephant.

"Dude, you are so awesome!" said Myah excitedly. Max grinned in response.

Tyler the elephant held a piece of paper in his trunk. He read, "A kid-sized volcano that anyone can make at home calls for 8 ounces of vinegar to be mixed with 2 tablespoons of baking soda. Myah, how much baking soda is in that bucket?"

"Uh, let me see. It says 200 tablespoons."

Tyler flapped his ears. "Hmmm, OK. So that would give us a volcano 100 times bigger than you might see in a home experiment."

He looked at Myah. The mouse looked at him. At the same time, they both shouted, "Awesome!"

"Is that big enough?" asked Johannah.

They nodded eagerly.

"You guys are really excited about this, aren't you?"

They nodded even more eagerly.

"Goblins are getting closer!" warned Jaydan.

"Mr. Awesome Troll," said Myah, "please dump the baking soda into the hole, if you would."

Max followed the instructions.

"Now, open up the barrel of vinegar. How much do we have in there?" asked Tyler.

"It says 1000 ounces," read Johannah. "Is that enough?"

"Well," reasoned Tyler, "if 2 tablespoons of baking soda calls for 8 ounces of vinegar, how much does 200 call for?"

Max shrugged and pointed at the barrel. "That much?"

"That's not very scientific of you," chided the elephant. "How did we go from 2 to 200?"

"We multiplied by 100," said Myah.

"So what do we get if we multiply 8 ounces by 100?"

"800," said Johannah confidently.

"And we have 1000?"

"Yes."

"That's too much," said Tyler thoughtfully. "We need to get rid of . . . how much?"

"1000 minus 800 is . . .," Myah did the subtraction in her little mouse head, "200!"

"Guys, goblins!" said Jaydan urgently.

"How are we going to get rid of 200 ounces of . . ."

Myah's question was answered by Max, who plunked his rocky head into the vat of vinegar and took one mighty slurp. He pulled his head out, wiped his mouth with his arm, and asked, "That enough?"

No one answered. They were all staring at the troll, wide-eyed and horrified.

"What, trolls like vinegar."

No one answered.

"Really, it's fine," Max assured them.

"Goblins!" shouted Jaydan.

The scientists shook out of their stupor and judged that Max had, in fact, slurped up about 200 ounces of vinegar – *which no person should ever, ever do!!* They quickly added the red food coloring and dish soap into the vinegar vat.

"Now we have to pour this vinegar mixture into the hole with the baking soda," said Tyler.

"Goblins, coming around the bend!" shouted Jaydan. "Do it now!"

Max heaved the vat of vinegar into the hole and everyone ran to a safe distance.

Red foam began to bubble out of the hole. It churned and hissed and burped as it reacted.

Then it shot up with incredible speed and flowed down the peak into the valley . . .

. . . and toward the horde of onrushing goblins.

The goblins took one look at the churning red mess flowing down the cliff side and remembered their old bedtime stories.

"Oh no, a volcano!" they shouted in fear before tossing down their clubs and running back the way they came.

It had worked!

Cheers rose up from the top of the peak. Johannah, Tyler and Myah jumped and high-fived (or, high-hooved). Max smiled happily. Jaydan did cheerful loop-the-loops in the sky.

After a lengthy celebration, Jaydan landed beside her friends. She looked conflicted.

"This doesn't feel right," she said.

Johannah nodded. "Yeah, now that you mention it, that was kind of mean. We scared them pretty bad."

"Not the way the Queen would have done it," grunted Max.

Heavy silence passed between them. It was only broken when Jaydan lifted off into the air.

"I'm going to apologize," she said. "I'll talk to them, try to find out exactly why they're invading. Maybe we can find a way to get along."

"Isn't that dangerous?" asked Myah, worried.

"Maybe," called Jaydan as she flew off. "Keep moving north. I'll find you later."

Max waved goodbye. Johannah kicked the ground a few times sadly.

Tyler sat down and looked at the red, foamy mess below. The red volcano foam was mingling with the orange toothpaste foam from their earlier experiment, making a pretty swirling pattern.

Pretty, but messy.

"So, ah," he said quietly, "who wants to get the mop?

9 A NEW FRIEND

Back in the tunnel, Izzy was tired. The torch-lit hallway seemed to run on forever with no end in sight. It was long and it was boring.

Michael tried to keep her spirits up with jokes and stories, but even his enthusiasm was flagging.

They had no way of knowing how long they had been in the tunnel. Long enough to be hungry, they reasoned. Both of their stomachs were growling loud enough for the other to hear.

As they walked, Michael flipped through the book Katelynn had tossed to them.

"It's mostly stories," he explained, "people guessing at what the treasure might be. No one is even sure how the tunnel got here."

"Maybe it's something that's been hidden from the dragon," thought Izzy, "which is why he sent the goblins to find it?"

"I'm seeing something about a door," he said.

"What kind of door?"

"I don't know," he admitted. "But it does say this: The bug and the bee must fly to be free, but all must stick together."

"That doesn't make any sense," Izzy complained.

Michael shrugged. "Maybe it will when we get to the door. If we ever get to the door."

Hours later, when they finally got to the door, they found they weren't the first to arrive.

A goblin was already there.

And he was not happy.

His wiry little body was tense. Sweat matted his orange-green hair to his head. His hands were fists and he was pounding on the solid stone door.

And what a door it was! Thick and heavy, it featured an imposing black framed arch. Ornate carvings of bugs and insects covered the surface of the door. The flickering torchlight in the hall made it look like the engraved creatures were moving.

Next to the door was a small stone shelf, and on it were a jumble of stone tiles. There were words written on them, but they were still too far away for Izzy or Michael to read.

Above the shelf were three distinct slots. They almost looked like keyholes.

The frustrated goblin still hadn't noticed their arrival, so Izzy broke the silence. "I'm sorry I tackled you," she said earnestly. "It wasn't the right thing to do."

The goblin jumped so high and so fast that he lost his balance and fell to the floor. He cracked his elbow on the frame of the door and yowled in pain. Then he glared at the knights with a look of sadness.

It was a deep sadness.

Rubbing his bruised elbow, he sighed. "I didn't want to be here, you know. None of this was my idea."

Michael sat down cross-legged on the floor a few feet away. "The dragon?"

"Of course the dragon!" snapped the goblin. He then calmed a little and took on a more reasonable tone. "I think he was hoping to find something useful down here."

"Like what?" asked Izzy, still standing a few feet away.

The goblin shook his sweaty head. "I don't know for sure. He asked me to stay behind and see what I could find. He left my friend with that creepy orb to distract everyone so I could get down here."

"How did you know where to look?" asked Michael.

"The dragon told us. I have no idea how he knew. I wasn't about to ask." The goblin shrugged. "But I guess it doesn't matter. I failed. I certainly can't fight two knights, and I can't get through that door by myself."

"We don't want to fight you," said Michael.

"We want to help you," said Izzy.

Scoffing, the goblin asked, "Why? Goblins aren't citizens of Maple. We live under the dragon's rule."

"Kindness knows no borders," said Izzy gravely.

The goblin looked at her oddly, as if he didn't believe her.

"She's right," said Michael. "We don't want to fight. We just want to get our Queen back."

They were quiet for a moment as the goblin considered what they had said.

"OK," he said at last. "How about this? The only way out is by going forward. We can't go back. So how about we work together to get to the treasure. I'll . . . I'll let you guys have it so you can trade it to the dragon in exchange for your Queen."

Michael smiled and nodded. "That sounds like a good plan. What's your name, friend?"

"Eduardo," he said.

Michael looked to Izzy, who nodded and smiled. He then offered his hand to the goblin.

"OK, Eduardo. We'll take that deal."

"Won't the dragon be mad at you?" asked Izzy.

Eduardo shrugged. "Sometimes you just have to do the right thing, even if it means a dragon might eat you."

Michael had already turned his attention to the door. "The bug and the bee must fly to be free, but all must stick together," he muttered to himself.

"What was that?" asked the goblin.

"From this book," said Michael, holding up the *Secrets of the Dragon's Treasure*.

Izzy pointed to the stone shelf and the small tiles. "Look at those," she said. "Three of the tiles say 'bug,' 'bee,' and 'fly'!"

Michael examined the tiles. Izzy was right. There were also three other tiles that said "bumble," "dragon," and "lady."

"Interesting," said Izzy. She pointed at the key slots. "I assume we have to pick the correct tiles and insert them in here?"

"Makes sense," said Michael. "And based on the book, the three correct tiles are bug, bee, and fly."

"Give it a try," replied Izzy hopefully.

Michael and Eduardo inserted the three tiles into the slots. There was a grinding noise, like rusty gears trying to turn. But the door did not budge.

And then the three tiles were ejected from the slots with force. They flew out and bounced off Michael's forehead.

"Ouch," he said, bending over to pick up the tiles. "I guess that was wrong."

"Maybe we put them in the wrong order?" asked Eduardo. So they tried a few different variations, but the result was the same each time.

"We're missing something," Michael said glumly as he gently rubbed his sore forehead.

Izzy was thinking. "What did the phrase say? The end of it, I mean."

"Um, let me see," said Michael, flipping through the book. ". . . But all must stick together."

"Stick together," she repeated. "All. That's weird phrasing." She thought for a moment, then snapped her fingers. "I've got it!"

"What?" asked Michael.

"What about compound words?" she said with a grin.

"I don't know what that means," said Eduardo, embarrassed.

"It's when you take two words and stick them together to make a new word. Like, for instance," she grabbed two of the tiles from the table, "'bumble' and 'bee.' Two separate words that, when put together, make a whole new word. Bumblebee."

Izzy tapped the two tiles together. There was a quiet click. They had stuck together.

"This way," said Izzy, connecting the other tiles, "*all* tiles are sticking together, just like the clue said. See, dragonfly and ladybug. They're all insects, see?"

"Genius," said Michael.

They slid the newly constructed word tiles into the three key slots. Again, they heard the grinding noise. But this time, the door began to slowly inch open.

"Woohoo!" shouted Eduardo, jumping up and down. Without thinking, he threw his arms around Izzy and Michael in a fierce hug.

They hugged back.

Making new friends was pretty great.

10 BONES!

The western road threaded inwards away from the sea. The northern mountains loomed on the horizon, and the terrain was getting steeper and rockier. The going was slower now that the travelling party had doubled in size.

Owen, Pat, Madison, and Stalin had talked with the goblins for a long time on the beach. It took some time, but they found common ground and realized they weren't that different from one another.

The goblins, for their part, were pretty great. They were thoughtful and funny and wise in their own way.

But mostly they were scared.

They were not invading the realm of Maple by choice. The dragon was forcing them to do that by using fear and intimidation. The goblins wished no harm on the peaceful citizens of Maple. In fact, the goblins were a little jealous of them.

Life in the goblin villages in the northern mountains was hard. Under the rule of the dragon, it was not a happy place. According to Flik, the leader of the three goblins who had joined their party, goblins are creative by nature. They love painting and singing and dancing. But the dragon cares only about work.

Flik feared the creative light inside every goblin was in danger of going out.

Owen was not about to let that happen.

Even Stalin the Seashell Knight, with all of his elaborate goblin traps, had come around. He had eagerly joined their party and ended up spending most of his time with the goblins, telling jokes and sharing stories. He had joined the group wearing an enormous backpack full of all manner of things – tools, wires, ropes, and countless little gadgets with unknown uses. He was quite the engineer.

So onward they travelled, farther and farther north, the sea disappearing while the mountains grew ahead of them.

At one point, Flik and his brothers, Stik and Wik, volunteered to scout ahead. They knew a larger force of goblins was in the area and didn't want their friends stumbling into trouble.

A few hours after the goblins departed, the companions came upon a curious sight. Near the side of the road, at the base of a tall, rocky hill, was a wide, deep pit. The sandy, dusty area was roped off with yellow rope. Old, dirt-covered bones were scattered about. Many had little labels on them. Others were piled up or laid out in rows. A few of the bones were taller than a person.

"Whoa, cool," said Stalin.

"Look at all those dinosaur bones," said Pat admiringly. "I love reading about dinosaurs."

Across the dig site, a head popped out from a deep hole. Though she was wearing thick goggles and was covered in dust, her face beamed with a smile.

"Hey, it's people!" she shouted happily. "And a giant snail! Wow! Hi, giant snail!"

Stripey bobbed his eyestalks in greeting.

The girl pulled herself out of the hole. She was wearing a rainbow-splashed shirt, a pair of shorts, and some oversized work boots. A tool belt, full of chisels and brushes and tiny hammers, hung across her hips,.

"Hi," she said, "I'm Doctor Violet, Paleontologist. I'm digging up dinosaur bones. You want one?"

Stalin nodded eagerly. He pointed to a femur bone that was twice his size.

Before Violet could answer, they were interrupted by urgent shouting from just over the hill. It was Flik, running down the road as fast as his short goblin legs could carry him. He skidded to a halt and tried to catch his breath.

"Flik, what is it?" asked Stalin.

"The other goblins, they won't listen. We tried to tell them that you are friendly, but they are too scared of the dragon. They're coming. They won't stop. I'm sorry, my friends."

The companions frowned with worry. Even Stripey seemed flustered. Despite Madison's attempts to calm him, the snail began inching around in circles and oozing more slime than usual.

Flik looked heartbroken. Pat placed a hand on his shoulder. "I'm sure you did your best, Flik. I'm proud of you."

"Stik and Wik are trying to slow them down, but it won't work. You need to run."

Owen turned to Violet. "We need to leave, Doctor. There's an army of goblins coming this way."

"Well? We can't leave!" said Violet stubbornly. "My work isn't done. Do you have any idea what an army of goblins would do to a dig site? Look around you. It's basically all sand. This is like a giant litter box to them."

"*Blurk*," blurked Pat, going a little green.

"Well that's unpleasant," said Stalin.

"Probably true, though," admitted Flik.

"*Blurk*," blurked Pat again.

"Be that as it may," said Owen sternly, "you can't stay."

Violet stomped her foot. "I can and I will. I need to protect my work. You guys look smart. Let's work together to try and figure something out."

The others shared a look and nodded. Stalin in particular seemed excited by the challenge.

Owen was more skeptical. He said, "Well, aside from a whole lot of bones, I don't see much we can . . ."

Violet interrupted him. "Wait, did you say a dragon sent the goblins? Hmmm. These are T-Rex bones," she said, thinking. "A T-Rex, in some ways, looks a lot like a dragon."

"Does it?" asked Owen doubtfully.

"I know a thing or two about goblins," continued Violet. "First and foremost, they've got terrible eyesight above ground."

Flik nodded. "We live in caves. The sun hurts our eyes."

Violet turned to Stalin, eyeing his backpack. "You seem to have come prepared. I assume you like to build things?

"I build lots of things," replied Stalin. "What do you have in mind?"

Violet picked up a small dinosaur skull from the ground, placed it on her head and said with a smile, "Rawr?"

"I don't follow," said Owen.

"I see what she's getting at," said Stalin excitedly, "but you're going to need a much bigger skull."

Violet took a few steps to her left, pulled at a dusty brown tarp, and revealed the gigantic skull of a full-grown T-Rex.

Stalin began to hop around, his shell vest jingling. "Oh, this is amazing. Doctor, you are brilliant! Yes, we can make this work. But it's going to take time. We're going to need to . . . whoa!"

Stalin slipped, as his hopping landed him in Stripey's slimy snail trail. "Madison, can't you keep him from getting this slippery goo all over the place?"

"Sorry! He gets extra slimy when he's nervous."

That gave Violet an idea. "They're coming over the hill, you say?"

"Yes, and soon," said Flik. "Within the hour."

Violet smiled and her eyes twinkled. "Then I know just what to do. Hey, giant snail, are you ready to make some giant snail slime?"

Stripey barked happily and nodded.

*   *   *

Wik and Stik were exhausted. They had been trying for hours to convince their goblin friends that the people of Maple were not their enemies. But few would listen. *The dragon says*, they all responded sadly.

The dragon says run.

The dragon says smash.

The dragon says destroy.

If only this goblin army had the chance to sit and talk to the brave Owen, the chill Madison, the kind Pat, and the quirky Stalin. They'd realize what Wik and Stik had already learned: *They don't have to listen to the dragon*.

But driven by fear, the goblins ran. They smashed. They destroyed. They would not listen to reason. They would not stop to talk.

They would stop, it turned out, for a hill covered in snail slime.

*   *   *

"It's working!" called Madison from the top of the hill. "They're slipping and sliding all over the place."

She had ridden Stripey up and down the hill as many times as they could, and had only just finished before the goblins appeared. Icky, gooey snail slime coated the entire tree-lined road. The goblins were gamely trying to run up the hill, but they kept slipping and falling back into a tangle at the bottom.

"They'll figure it out soon," said Flik from just behind her. "Once they stop and think about it, they'll realize that they can just run up the side through the trees. But this'll buy us some time, at least."

"I hope this works," said Madison, looking back towards the dig site.

*   *   *

The dig site was very active.

Under the joint direction of Dr. Violet and Stalin, Owen and Pat were assembling bones, stringing wire, and gathering leaves and branches. It was an excellent display of teamwork.

First, they built the skeleton. It towered over them, more than twenty feet tall. With massive legs, tiny arms, and a skull big enough to fit a human, the T-Rex skeleton was impressive.

Using supplies from his backpack, Stalin rigged a series of pulleys and levers. The wires and cords wound around the jaw, arms, and legs of the beast. They all came together into one confusing jumble in the ribcage of the skeleton, where Stalin was perched on a makeshift chair. He tugged one lever, and the jaw opened. He pulled another and an arm moved.

While he practiced his skeleton driving, the others were working on building the dragon's skin by layering the bones with leaves and branches.

It wasn't perfect. In fact, it looked exactly like what it was – a skeleton covered in leaves.

"I'm not sure if this is going to work," said Pat.

"Let's try it out on our test subject," said Violet. "Flik," she called, "what do you think?"

The goblin looked back from the top of the hill and squinted. His face betrayed his true feelings. "I mean, it *almost* looks like a dragon."

"Not good enough," said Violet. She looked up at the sky, feeling the warmth of the bright midday sun on her face. Then she snapped her fingers.

"You just had an idea," noted Owen.

"Give me your armor," she said. "You, too, Pat. And your giant shield, too."

The knights were perplexed.

"A horde of angry goblins is coming and you want us to take *off* our armor?" asked Owen.

"Trust me, I'm a paleontologist," was Violet's answer.

And they did trust her. Under her direction, they shed their armor and placed it, along with Pat's shield, behind the not-quite-a-dragon.

The sun glinted off the shiny metal, creating a bright reflection behind the skeleton.

"Perfect," she said. "How about now, Flik?"

The goblin turned and quickly took a step back, forgetting for a moment what he was seeing. With the bright light behind the skeleton blinding him a little, it really did kind of almost look like a dragon.

"I think that'll work," said Madison. "And it'll have to, because the goblins are coming!"

She moved Stripey away from the hill and hid behind a cluster of rocks.

"Wait!" shouted Stalin from inside the skeleton. "Someone needs to do the voice!"

"I'll do it," said Owen, making a move to climb up into the skeleton's mouth. But Pat stopped him.

"No," he said. "Let me."

"Are you sure? It could be dangerous?"

"I'm sure," he said bravely.

Owen clapped him on the back and helped him climb up into the dinosaur's mouth. Pat tucked himself in, more than a little uncomfortable.

"I know I'm not being eaten by a T-Rex," said Pat, "but it sure feels like I am."

Violet and Owen wished him luck and scurried off to hide.

The goblins, howling and raging, crested the hill and came face to face with their biggest fear in the whole wide world.

The dragon!

Or something that looked almost like a dragon if they didn't look too hard.

Flik tried to help sell the ruse by easing to the front of the stricken goblin horde and falling to his knees.

"Oh, great dragon master, tell us your command!" he shouted loudly.

But the dragon said nothing.

"That's your cue, kid," whispered Stalin, who made ready to open and close the jaw.

"Oh, right," said Pat. Clearing his throat, he shouted in his deepest dragon voice, "Er, um, hey guys. How's things?"

Behind a rock, Owen whispered, "We're dead."

"Give him a chance!" snapped Violet.

"Oh great dragon," called Flik, "we have come to smash and destroy as you have commanded. Is that – um, have you maybe changed your mind about that?"

"Er, yes," boomed dragon-Pat, "I have. Yeah, so, forget what I said about all that, okay. No more smashing, no more destroying. Let's all, I don't know, try to be nice to each other . . . and stuff."

Some of the goblins looked skeptical. Others were clearly pleased. This all seemed pretty weird, though.

"Tell you what," said dragon-Pat, "if you all leave your clubs and sticks and whatnot here, you can go on down the road a little bit. You'll come to a beach. It's a really fine beach. Just relax, maybe build some sand castles. Hey, did any of you happen to bring a Frisbee?"

The goblins looked confused. They muttered back and forth to each other. This was getting weirder and weirder. But luckily, one goblin in the back raised his hand. In it was a small, pink Frisbee.

"OK, great, sweet," said dragon-Pat. "Have a game of Frisbee on the beach. Just, you know, chill. I'm going to send some friends to meet you. One is this really fun guy, wears seashells on his head and stuff. *Totally* crazy dude. The other is this scientist who . . . well, whatever, she's smart and nice. Anyway, they're going to come talk to you. We don't want to fight anymore, you know? I mean, *they* don't. I mean, just listen to what they have to say, OK?"

The goblins gathered together and conversed. They talked for a while. They argued a little. Some even laughed once or twice. After a long conversation, they reached a consensus.

Flik stepped forward.

"They know you aren't the real dragon," he admitted.

Pat panicked. He started to breathe faster and his face grew red. His shoulders were tense. *I should have let someone else do it*, he thought.

"But," continued Flik with a grin, "this is the most entertaining thing we've seen in years. So we're going to head to the beach and play some Frisbee. Forget the dragon. We want to be friends."

Pat sighed as the tension left his body. He laughed, and the goblins laughed with him.

So the goblins dropped their weapons and agreed to head to the beach. They would meet with the people of Maple. They would talk.

They would listen.

*   *   *

Later, after Flik led the goblins away to the beach, Madison and the knights said their goodbyes to Stalin and Doctor Violet.

"You two will be okay dealing with the goblins?" asked Sir Owen.

Violet nodded. "Of course. They're sweethearts. In fact, I'm thinking of hiring them to help me at the dig site. I could use some student interns. These mountains are full of fossils."

Hugs were exchanged, and Violet and Stalin departed south. Owen and Pat put their armor back on and took up position in front of Madison and Stripey.

The base of Dragon Mountain lay just ahead.

11 THE SCHOOL ON VIEW HILL

The forest road wound through lush foliage, quaint villages, and quiet vistas. It was serene and beautiful. The realm of Maple was truly a marvel to behold.

"Stupid trees," muttered Jackson. "Stupid rivers and streams. Stupid road."

"Don't say stupid," mumbled Madi, who was half-asleep on the knight's shoulder. "It's not a kind word."

Katelynn, still tucked under Jackson's arm, snored a little otter snore.

"*Stupid* goblins," said Jackson, as if daring Madi to argue. She didn't.

The goblins were still on their tail. Despite help from each village they passed, Jackson and his companions still couldn't shake their pursuers. The goblins were relentless.

Step after step he trudged onward, lost in a dream of better times. His eyes glazed.

The tired knight didn't even notice the troll until he walked into her.

"Oof," he said.

"Young man," barked the troll, "helmets off in the school!"

Reflexively, Jackson whipped off his helmet and flung it away. It went clattering into the bushes. The noise woke up Katelynn and Madi.

The gray troll was standing in the middle of the road at the base of a mossy green stone bridge. Beyond the bridge on a rounded hill was a unique sight – a collection of colorful geometric shapes stuck together to make a school.

The School at View Hill.

They had finally reached Preposition Bridge. They were nearly to the base of Dragon Mountain.

Katelynn, ever the librarian, hopped down in excited fascination. "Ooh, I've always wanted to visit this place. It's the best school in all of Maple."

"Just so," said the troll. "And I'm the gatekeeper, Marti. What's your business here?"

Katelynn, Jackson, and Madi blurted it all out at once: from the kidnapping of the Queen, to the goblin invasion, to the chase through the forest. Marti tried to keep up, but eventually rolled her eyes and let them pass.

"Go on, go on," she said. "Go find Diggins in Verb Hall. She'll help you." To Madi, she said, "And don't you be getting that pixie dust everywhere. I'm not cleaning that up!"

Madi nodded, and then tried to catch the wayward specks of pixie dust that fell from her head. Marti waved her away with a grumble.

Katelynn thanked the troll profusely as she traversed the bridge. Jackson made a move to retrieve his helmet, but a glare from the troll sent him scurrying over the bridge.

"I'm retiring tomorrow," she grumbled as the trio passed. "I can't believe I'm dealing with this on my last day."

After a short walk up the hill, the companions reached the doors to Verb Hall. The hall was a massive red sphere. Stretching out from the sphere was a series of arched, green walkways and pink rectangular corridors. They led to a number of blue and black pyramid-shaped structures and smaller pink spheres.

The hall was empty. Yet still, it was full of activity. The engraved interior wall of the sphere was adorned with moving images of action. Brought to life by magic, each etching and carving moved in a lifelike manner, depicting people jumping, running, swimming, cooking, and climbing. If you could imagine someone doing something, you could find it on the animated interior of the Verb Hall.

"Wow," breathed Madi, entranced.

The floor at their feet began to shift. With little warning, a neatly dressed mole popped up through the floor, sending mounds of dirt in every direction.

"Greetings, travelers," she said warmly. "I'm Diggins, the Program Director of View Hill. Marti tells me you have a goblin problem?"

Once again, the companions began talking all at once, recounting their journey in rambling detail. Diggins held up two tiny mole paws and silenced the room.

"Don't worry, you'll be safe here, and we'll get you on your way to saving the Queen in no time flat. But first, there are some things I'd like to show you. Head down the If Corridor, please."

Diggins pointed to a pink hallway on the right, then leapt up and dove back into her burrow hole. The companions shrugged, confused, but followed her instructions.

At the end of the pink corridor (which was wallpapered with the word "If" over and over and over again), Diggins popped up out of the floor again.

Jackson pointed at the hole in the floor and asked, "Why don't you just walk?"

Diggins raised an eyebrow. "Why don't you just burrow?"

The knight had no answer for that and the mole wasn't expecting one.

"Follow me," she said. She opened the door at the end of the hallway. It opened into a pyramid-shaped classroom. There were no desks, just a number of students sitting in a circle on the floor. They all had mats laid out in front of them. It was snack time.

Diggins entered the room and called out three names. "Amaya, Avaya, Alaya, please come here."

Three small goblins in flowered dresses scurried up and rushed over to Diggins. Jackson, Madi, and Katelynn were dumbstruck.

"Those are . . ." began Jackson.

"Three of our best students," said Diggins curtly. "Isn't that right, girls?"

The goblin girls nodded and smiled. Diggins patted them on their heads and sent them back to their snacks.

The mole closed the classroom door and turned to the knight, otter and pixie.

"We don't get many goblins here. They tend to stay in their caves – most likely because they're afraid of making the dragon mad. But when some do come down, they integrate just like anyone else. By the end of the standard normalization period, they're just like the rest of their classmates. I know you are having some trouble with the goblins right now, but I want you to see that they aren't any different than you or me. Back in the old days, before the gray men, all creatures lived in harmony together. Goblins were no different than pixies or otters or humans."

"But they kidnapped our Queen!" protested Madi.

"And they've been chasing us for-*EVER*!" complained Jackson.

"Have they?" asked Diggins. "Are you sure? Maybe they were looking for your help? Did you talk to them?"

Jackson shook his head.

To Madi, Diggins said, "And yes, they did help the dragon take Helen. But why? Have you given any thought to that?"

Madi frowned. She hadn't.

Katelynn had, though. "The dragon is a bully. He rules the goblins like the old gray men used to rule us. The goblins aren't doing this because they want to. They're doing it because they're afraid of what will happen if they don't."

Diggins smiled and nodded. "Let's get you three some warm food and warm beds. You can eat, rest, and then be on your way. We'll handle the goblins that are following you."

They all thought that was a great idea. Within the hour, all three had full stomachs and were sleeping soundly.

*   *   *

When they left View Hill a few hours later, resupplied and re-energized, they noticed five goblins kicking a soccer ball around the lawn.

"We should talk to them," said Katelynn.

Jackson and Madi nodded.

They approached the goblins cautiously. The goblins eyed the trio warily.

"Um," said Katelynn, unsure of herself.

But that was enough for the goblins. They all began chattering at once. They apologized for everything. It was the dragon, they said, who made them jump through the scary portal. They had no wish to fight the citizens of Maple.

"And we weren't chasing you," one of them finally said. "We were running away. We knew this school was a safe place for goblins."

"You shouldn't have had those squirrels throw rocks at us," said another.

"We're real sorry about that," said Katelynn. "We're sorry about all of it."

"All of Maple should be safe for you," said Jackson.

"We're going to make sure that it is," said Madi firmly.

After conversing for a while longer, the new friends departed with handshakes and hugs. Katelynn, Madi, and Jackson continued their trek north, determined to make a difference.

12 THE TREASURE OF FRIENDSHIP

The underground tunnel seemed endless.

Izzy, Michael, and Eduardo were too tired and too hungry to talk. Sometimes they stopped and rested, but resting just made them think about how hungry they were.

So they kept walking.

Eduardo shared what little food he found in his pockets. Roots mostly, from a scrawny mountain tree that goblins ate. It was bitter and unpleasant and it did little to drive away their hunger.

"The book doesn't say anything about how long the tunnel is, does it?" asked Izzy.

Michael shook his head. "This book says a whole lot of nothing."

"But it helped you light the torches," said Eduardo, "and open the insect door. I think it's already said a fair amount."

"Here, then," said Michael, tossing the book to the goblin in frustration.

Eduardo caught the book but seemed uneasy holding it. He began to sweat a little, and his eyes became moist.

Michael paused a moment. "Oh. You can't read, can you?" he asked gently.

The goblin shook his head sadly. "Most goblins can't. We aren't allowed to learn. Some sneak off to View Hill for school, but I was never able to."

Michael put a gentle hand on his friend's shoulder. "Don't worry, pal. We'll teach you. We can teach all of you."

"Guys!" exclaimed Izzy. "Look!"

Just up ahead, the tunnel widened into a vast cavern. The floor sloped down sharply and dropped off into a bottomless chasm. Similarly, the ceiling rose up into the darkness. On the other side of the cavern was a torch-lit doorway, and the only way across the expanse was a stone bridge. It looked solid and safe.

"Maybe we're finally getting to the end," offered Eduardo hopefully.

"I hope there's some pizza on the other side," said Izzy as her stomach growled.

"Pizza?" asked Eduardo. "What is pizza?"

"You've never had pizza?!" shouted both Izzy and Michael at the same time.

"Nope. Is it good?"

The knights shook their heads in disbelief. They were going to have some serious words with the dragon about this.

Exactly halfway across the bridge, the trio came to a curious sight. A series of oddly colored stones stretched across the width of the bridge. There were four rows of nine stones, and each stone had a number etched onto its surface. Each stone in the first row showed the number one. The second row showed tens. The third showed hundreds. And the fourth row featured thousands.

"This is odd," said Izzy. "You see anything in the book about this?"

Michael retrieved the book from Eduardo. "I don't think so. Certainly nothing about a stone bridge."

He began flipping through the book quickly, looking for something helpful.

"Maybe we should just walk across," suggested Eduardo.

"That seems risky," answered Izzy.

Eduardo waved her off. "Come on, they're just stones. What's the worst that could happen?"

The little goblin moved forward. He stepped on one of the squares in the first row. The square lit up with a dull yellow glow.

"OK," he said cringing, "maybe this wasn't a good idea after all."

He took another cautious step forward, landing on a 10 square. It lit up a dark red, as did the rest of the squares in all four rows.

"Uh oh."

Every square on the board instantly jerked up, as if on tightly coiled springs, and launched the poor little goblin backwards towards his friends. He plowed into Michael and they tumbled to the ground.

The stones then settled back to their normal places, looking completely harmless.

"Sorry about that," said Eduardo, as he untangled himself from Michael.

Michael tried to speak, but his helmet had gotten turned around and was covering his face. It was firmly stuck. Izzy yanked the helmet off his head with a grunt.

"Thanks," he said. "What I was trying to say was that I may have found something."

"I told you that book was useful," said Eduardo.

Michael held up the book and read, "To cross the Bridge of Numbers, you must count the hairs on a goblin's head."

Michael and Izzy turned and looked at Eduardo and his messy, sweaty hair. There was no way they could accurately count that mess. Nor did they want to.

The goblin laughed.

"It's a goblin fable," he said with a smile. "Legend says that every goblin child is born with 2432 hairs on their head. It's just a story, since I've seen totally bald goblin babies, but that's what the old folks tell us."

"Weird," said Izzy.

"The weirdness of goblin mythology aside, we seem to have our answer," said Michael.

Eduardo was skeptical. "But how does that help us cross the bridge?"

"That's easy," said Michael, moving towards the squares. "You see how each square has a number, right?"

"Oh, I sure do," said Eduardo, rubbing his bruised head.

"You just need to step on the squares to add up to 2432."

Izzy nodded. "Oh, well done, Michael! Very thoughtful."

Eduardo still didn't understand. "I don't see a 2432 square, though."

"Nope, but we can add up to it. We start with units, which is the first position on the right. How many units are there in the number 2432?"

"Two," said Izzy.

So just as Eduardo had done, Michael stepped onto a 1 square. It lit up a dull yellow. But instead of stepping forward to the next row, Michael took a step sideways onto a second 1 square.

He held his breath until it, too, lit up yellow. He sighed in relief.

"Now, next is the tens spot. What's the number in the tens spot of 2432?"

They waited for the goblin to answer, but he still didn't understand.

"Three," said Izzy. "So that means you need to step on three blocks in that row.

Michael stepped forward onto a 10 square and then stepped sideways onto two more. Three 10 squares glowed yellow.

The goblin clapped and jumped happily. "I think I'm starting to understand. On the next row, you need to step on four squares to total 400, right?"

"Good work, Eduardo," said Izzy.

"And then you step on two squares in the last row to make 2000?"

"Yes!"

Eduardo laughed and laughed. "I can do math!" he shouted in glee.

Michael activated the four 100 squares and then jumped forward to trigger the two 1000 squares. As his foot hit the second 1000 square, all the blocks began to tremble.

"Uh oh," he said, tensing.

But all was well. All the squares on the board lit up a bright, pleasant green. Michael cheered and hopped off the board onto the other side.

With only a little hesitation, Izzy and Eduardo raced across.

"We couldn't have done it without you," Izzy said to Eduardo.

"And I couldn't have done it without you," he said. "We make a good team."

So, on they walked.

Not far beyond the bridge, they came to a small room. Resting on a pedestal in the center of the tight space was the treasure. Beyond the treasure was a stairway leading up. The way out.

The treasure was not what they were expecting.

It was not gold, or silver, or jewels, or gems. It wasn't magic, or a weapon, or a giant pizza, either – though no one would have complained about treasure pizza.

No, this treasure was better than that.

It was the answer to all of their problems. It was a way to free the Queen and bring peace back to not just Maple, but also to the goblins in the mountains.

Ever so carefully, Izzy took the treasure in her hands and the friends hurried up the stairs.

They had to save the day.

13 THE FROST FAIRIES

The air became colder as Jaydan soared deeper into the mountains in search of the fleeing goblins.

She considered turning back, finding Max and Johannah and continuing with them to Dragon Mountain. But something stopped her.

Was it guilt at how they had scared the goblins with the baking-soda-and-vinegar volcano? Or was there something more?

An icy cold gust of wind hit her then, causing her to shiver. That's when she noticed that it had started snowing.

It should not have been snowing here. She wasn't far enough up into the mountains, and it was still early autumn. Something wasn't right.

But the wind carried more than snow. It carried voices. Goblin voices.

Goblin cries for help.

Jaydan flapped her broad wings and soared down, following the calls for help. But after a moment, the voices stopped. She looked around, panicked. Where were they?

That's when she saw the bubble.

It was huge – larger than the Queen's castle – but clear, like it was made of glass. And it was FULL of terrified goblins slowly bobbing up and down and all around. They floated in a sparkling liquid that looked like water filled with glitter.

Like a goblin snow globe.

Jaydan landed in a broad clearing at the base of the eerie, goblin-filled bubble. To her left was a small copse of trees. It looked like many of the trees were damaged. The brush underfoot was trampled.

She tapped the surface of the snow globe with a hoof. It was solid like glass, but it rippled like water. And it was very, very cold.

A small cyclone of wind, snow, and ice swirled in front of her. The icy particles crystallized into two distinct figures: two tiny, giggling frost fairies. They wore dresses made of snowflakes and had small wings made of ice. They wore icicle crowns and their eyes were a deep blue.

"Look, Ariana, a horse with wings," said one of the fairies.

"I see it, Addison," replied Ariana. "Fly along, horsey, unless you want to buy a ticket to our show."

The Pegasus snorted and stomped a foot. "I am Jaydan, Royal Steed of Helen, the

Queen of Grace and Courtesy. What exactly is going on here?"

The fairies giggled, unimpressed.

"We made a snow globe," said Addison.

"A very pretty snow globe," said Ariana.

"We take ugly things and make them pretty," said Addison. "That's what frost fairies do. We come in winter and decorate your lifeless trees with ice and snow. We bring beauty."

Ariana pointed to the bubble filled with drifting, crying goblins. "And nothing is uglier than big, nasty goblins. But see how pretty we made them? They won't cause any trouble in there, will they?"

Jaydan scowled, but she tamped down her anger and tried to be empathetic, remembering the nearby destruction she had noticed. "Is this your home? Did the goblins cause this mess when they came down the mountain road?"

A shadow crossed over Addison's face. "Oh yes, they did. They tore our land up from bush to bough and were gone before we could stop them."

"But then they came back," said Ariana with a giggle. "They came scurrying back shouting and crying and running in fear. And we were ready for them this time, weren't we, Addison?"

The frost fairies giggled and danced.

"This isn't our way," said Jaydan coldly. "This is not how we treat others. It doesn't matter that they're goblins. Everyone should be treated with dignity and respect."

Ariana shot forward and pointed an icy finger at Jaydan. "Tell that to the monsters who destroyed our home!"

Jaydan sighed. "I know it's not always easy to do the right thing. Sometimes, all you want to do is lash out and attack someone for what they've done. But does that ever solve anything? Do two wrongs ever make a right?"

Addison shrugged. "Well, they won't be stomping any more homes cooped up in there. Seems like we're doing *some*thing right."

"But at what cost?" asked Jaydan. "Look at them. They're suffering. Does inflicting pain and misery on those goblins somehow bring your homes back?"

After a quick glance at one another, the fairies admitted that it did not.

"So how have you solved anything?"

"I guess we haven't, really" said Ariana, glumly.

"Do you feel good about what you've done?" asked the Pegasus.

"We did until *you* showed up," Addison mumbled.

Ariana frowned. "They don't look very happy, do they?"

Addison sighed and asked, "Maybe we could ask them to help us rebuild?"

"That would be a good start," said Jaydan encouragingly. "Whatever you decide to do, talk it out first. Find out why they came down the mountain and smashed your homes. Seeing things from their perspective will help you understand them. That's called empathy. And having empathy for others improves relationships and fosters peace. That's what the Queen teaches us."

"OK, fine," said Ariana. "We'll let them out. But if they try anything . . ." she waggled icy fingers, sending snowy sparks into the air.

And so the fairies freed the goblins, and they all sat down and had a talk. The goblins apologized. They hadn't meant to wreck the fairy homes, but with the houses so small and so many goblins being forced to march south, damage was inevitable. The goblins agreed to help the fairies repair the damage they had caused.

The fairies also apologized to the goblins for their cruel reaction. They admitted that they had acted out of anger and had made a bad decision.

Proud of the fairies, Jaydan then made her own apologies to the goblins. She asked them to forgive her and her friends for scaring them with the volcano. The goblins accepted her apology and were relieved to hear that the volcano was nothing more than an oversized science experiment.

They also agreed to head back north to Dragon Mountain. They had lost the taste for invading. Not that they had much taste for it anyway. They were just doing what the dragon told them to do. They wanted to go home and be left alone. After the day they'd had, between volcanoes and snow globes, they were done doing the dragon's bidding.

With a promise to meet the goblins later and travel north with them, Jaydan left the clearing in search of her companions.

After hours and hours of searching, she noticed movement near the mouth of a small cave. She was surprised to find Captain Izzy, Sir Michael, and a friendly-looking goblin emerging from an underground cavern.

But she was more surprised to see what they were holding.

After a hurried reunion, the two knights and the goblin scampered onto Jaydan's back. Determining it was best to allow Max and Johannah to continue on their own, Jaydan took off without delay for Dragon Mountain.

14 MARCH OF THE GOBLINS

The Heroes of Maple were beginning to come together at the base of Dragon Mountain.

Owen, Pat, and Madison arrived first and scouted the area. It was not promising. There were only two ways up the mountain.

The first was travelling a long, winding path that weaved past the caves where the goblins lived. But that path would leave them exposed to whatever the dragon wanted to throw at them.

The second option was scaling a steep, dangerous cliff that was hundreds of feet high.

While Pat was staring up at the cliff face, turning positively green with the thought of trying to scale it, Katelynn, Jackson, and Madi arrived. They greeted their friends with hugs and smiles, and Madi was quickly pressed into service. At Owen's behest, she took off in a swirl of pixie dust and went to scout the higher reaches of the mountain.

"The dragon is asleep," she said when she returned, "at the very top of the winding path. The Queen is there, too. She's in a small wooden cage, guarded by goblins."

"Stripey can scale that cliff, no problem," said Madison. "He can even carry a few of us up, too. We can sneak in, grab the Queen, and then climb back down."

Jackson shook his head. "It won't work. The goblins will be sure to wake up the dragon before we escape. We'll never get away."

"We need a distraction," said Owen.

Luckily, a distraction soon presented itself in the form of not one, but two goblin armies.

From the west came a determined crowd of goblins led by Violet the Paleontologist, Stalin the Seashell Knight, and Flik. Not content to stay on the beach, the goblins came to confront the dragon and help the people of Maple.

"We talked, and we listened," said Violet, recounting her time on the beach with the goblins. "They want to be our friends."

From the east came Max and Johannah, who had never reconnected with Jaydan, but did come across the goblin army that she had rescued from the frost fairies. The goblins were eager to help the rock troll and the unicorn reach Dragon Mountain.

So the now rather large group came together to figure out the best way to get them all up the mountain. In the end, it was determined that Madison and the knights would ride Stripey up the back of the mountain, sneak in, and attempt to free the Queen.

To make sure they went unnoticed, the goblins bravely volunteered to organize a march up the winding path. Max, Johannah, Katelynn, Violet, and Stalin would accompany them.

*   *   *

Despite the dangers, the goblins marched.

They did so calmly and peacefully.

They brought no weapons, which made many of them nervous. They had only their voices, which rang out with pride, "Freedom! Freedom! Freedom!"

Before long, it became clear that the march was not only a convenient distraction to aid in the rescue of the Queen. No, it became so much more. It became a movement. Goblins, repressed and beaten down for so long, were rising up to take back their freedom.

As they marched, their numbers grew. Their bravery and passion inspired other goblins to come down out of their mountain caves. Soon, the entire goblin nation was on that winding path, marching hand-in-hand.

It was a sight to see.

Hopefully the dragon wouldn't eat them all.

*   *   *

On the back of the mountain, Stripey climbed. His powerful snail foot inched up the side of the cliff. Madison sat in her customary spot on the snail's shell, though she did grip the reins a little more tightly. Harnessed behind in various degrees of discomfort were Sirs Jackson, Owen, and Pat. The pixie was hiding at the top of the cliff, watching to make sure they weren't noticed.

The knights felt naked. They had left their swords, shields, and armor behind. It would have made them too heavy for the snail to haul.

From the back of the line, Pat called, "I feel sick."

"Don't look down," called Jackson to his companion.

"Looking at the sky makes me dizzy," said Pat.

"So don't look up either," said Owen, who was enjoying the climb.

"*Shhh*," hissed Madison. "We're supposed to be sneaky, remember?"

The knights closed their mouths. They still had a ways to go.

* * *

Helen, the Queen of Grace and Courtesy, awoke from a short nap to the sound of thousands of goblins chanting, "Freedom! Freedom! Freedom!"

That was unexpected.

Her time in the dragon's cell had been uneventful. Her goblin guards had treated her with respect – even friendliness – but the dragon had mostly ignored her. She had never even been told why she had been kidnapped.

In fact, the dragon spent most of his time in his cave, hidden from sight. He only came out to take naps in the sun.

His plan was obvious, though. Capture the Queen, and Maple would go to war to free her. Once again, the realm would be torn apart.

Why, she thought. *How does the dragon benefit from that?*

He wouldn't, was her next thought.

She had an idea of who would benfit, though. And she knew their plan would fail.

She knew her people well. She had taught them well. There would be no war.

But as she saw thousands of goblins peacefully marching up the road — well, she didn't realize she had taught them *that* well.

As the march reached the top of the mountain, the dragon started to stir.

*   *   *

"Freedom! Freedom! Freedom!" chanted the goblins. The leading cluster of marchers had reached the top. Curled up in a giant, scaly ball was the dragon.

"He's big," said Katelynn softly. She was sitting on Johannah's back, clutching the unicorn's soft rainbow mane with her otter paws.

The dragon stretched his wide, gray wings. His blue scales rippled in the sunlight. His mouth gaped open in a terrifying yawn — letting out a little bit of dragon drool. His eyes blinked open.

The dragon saw the goblins marching towards him.

The dragon roared.

"What! Is! This!"

For the first time since the march began, the goblins were stricken with doubt. What were they doing here? They couldn't stand up to a dragon! He was too big, too strong, too mean.

They were afraid.

The dragon raged. "I am Leo the Fierce, Leo the Powerful, Leo the Mighty! Who dares disturb me?!"

The goblins looked ready to run. Someone needed to rally them.

Mustering her courage, Katelynn hopped off the unicorn's back and stepped forward. She cleared her throat and spoke.

"Ahem, Mister Dragon, sir. I need to be honest. I'm really, really scared of you. You're very big and very scary and I am very, very scared. I would rather be just about anywhere else in the world than standing here in front of you.

"But here I am, Mister Dragon, because being afraid is not an excuse for inaction. You kidnapped our Queen. You've been terrorizing the goblins for years. We're here, scared and afraid, to tell you that it all has to stop."

Seeing someone so small and harmless standing up for them made the goblins feel brave again. They clapped and cheered and shouted support.

The dragon chuckled.

"Little otter, you are brave, and your words are sweet," he growled, "but what is your plan to stop me?"

Katelynn spread her arms wide and took another step forward. "That's the best part, Mister Dragon. We literally have *no* plan. None. We don't have a secret weapon or some master trick up our sleeve. We are completely at your mercy. You could belch your dragon fire, stomp us into bits, eat us one by one, and we could do nothing to stop you. Yet still, here we are."

The dragon thought for a moment, then began to move his massive head down to the ground to face Katelynn.

"You are right, little otter," he said with a cruel smile. "I can eat you. I can eat all of you. And maybe that's just what I'll do."

15 SHADES OF GRAY

"Hurry up, hurry up," chirped Madi, waving her arms frantically.

The knights had just arrived at the top of the mountain. Jackson and Owen looked around warily. Sir Pat hugged and kissed the rocky ground.

Jackson heard the thunderous snarl of the dragon. He spun around and saw the great beast moving towards his friend the otter.

"What's happening with Katelynn?" asked Jackson, reaching for a sword that was no longer hanging at his hip.

Madi saw it, too.

"Help the Queen!" she shouted as she dashed through the air towards the dragon.

And help her they did. With the guards distracted, it was an easy thing to smash the cage lock with a rock. Helen emerged from the cell, her cloak shimmering and her smile wide.

Her eyes went not to the dragon but to his cave. She needed to know what was in there.

"Stay here," she said as she strode purposefully into the darkness.

*   *   *

I'm going to be eaten, thought Katelynn as the dragon moved towards her. She was surprisingly calm about it.

The dragon opened his mouth. His breath stank. His teeth, yellow and green and huge and sharp, loomed before her.

And then, without warning, a pixie landed on the dragon's snout.

"Hi," Madi said, "Want to be friends?"

Leo the dragon reared back and roared, futilely swiping his arms at the fluttering pixie. She was way too fast. She just kept dashing off and landing back on his nose. He clamped his jaws open and shut, but she evaded every bite.

Soon, his entire snout was covered in pixie dust.

So of course, he sneezed.

It was a dragon-sized sneeze.

The force of the sneeze knocked hundreds of goblins to the ground. It threw the dragon backwards, too, causing him to trip and sit down heavily. He wiped furiously at his nose, which was dripping.

"I'm sorry about that," said Madi, "but it's not nice to eat people. Especially librarians!"

The dragon sniffed and snuffed. "I wasn't *really* going to eat her," he whined, "I was just trying to scare her."

"That's not any better," chided Johannah.

"Scaring people is not right," said Violet.

The dragon gurgled, cleared his throat, and then growled in frustration.

"But we're enemies!" he shouted. "The people of Maple hate the goblins and they hate dragons. They hate me! That is the way of things. It's how it's always been."

Katelynn looked confused. "Who told you that?"

"They did," sneered the dragon, pointing to the dark cave.

And there, emerging from the cave was the Queen, herding a group out of the shadows. The gray men. The old rulers of Maple. Helen's magical cloak was a swirling, living thing that helped to push and prod the reluctant villains into the light. They stumbled and hissed in dismay.

It had been them all along. They were behind the kidnapping.

The oldest, grayest man stepped forward and addressed Leo. "You see?" he hissed, "they came to attack you, just like we said! Destroy them, Leo! Destroy them all!"

Leo snarled, but he wavered. There was doubt in his eyes. Sure, the goblins had marched to confront him, but the otter was right. They didn't really seem like much of a threat.

Pat stepped forward then, with Jackson and Owen behind him. "We are Knights of Peace, sworn protectors of the Queen. We come before you with no sword, no shield, and no armor. Does that seem like an attack?"

Flik the goblin stepped forward. "We are the goblin people. We come before you with no weapons, no anger, and no hate. We come simply to talk, to show you that there is another way. Does that seem like an attack?"

Katelynn, the brave little otter, stepped forward. "I'm a harmless little otter. I work in a library. If this was an attack, would I even be here?"

Confusion shook Leo. All his life, the gray men had been telling him that the people of Maple hated him. And he had believed them, because it was all he knew.

But the people of Maple had come in peace, even after all he'd done. That didn't make any sense to the dragon.

So he dealt with the confusion in the only way he knew how, the way the gray men had taught him.

He shouted.

"NO!" he roared, and flames belched from his mouth into the sky. It was a terrifying sight.

The goblins scattered.

The knights cowered.

The gray men smiled.

And then the sky went dark as the broad wings of a Pegasus momentarily blocked out the setting sun. Swooping in gracefully, Jaydan landed softly in front of the dragon. She had a goblin and two knights on her back.

"Sorry we're late," apologized Jaydan, casting a sour glance back at Michael. "We had to stop and clean up."

Michael cringed. "I said I was sorry! I've never ridden a Pegasus before. I had no idea I'd get air-sick!"

"Three times," mumbled Izzy.

"Leo!" shouted Eduardo as he dismounted, clutching something under his arm.

Leo glared at him, but then a subtle flicker of hope passed over the dragon's angry face.

"You've always doubted the teaching of the gray men," said Eduardo. "That's why you left me at the castle to search their library for the secret passage. You heard the rumors of the tunnel, and you hoped it was true. Well, it was."

Eduardo held up the treasure. It was a scroll, ancient and cracked.

"I can't read . . . not yet, at least . . . but my new friends here read it to me. This treasure — it's a true history of the realm of Maple."

Izzy pointed at the gray men. "They did all this," she called. "They corrupted everything. For centuries, we all lived in peace. Humans, goblins, magical folk, even dragons. We *ALL* lived in peace."

"Then the gray men came," said Michael. "They divided us. They taught us to fear our differences, not embrace them. Instead of celebrating diversity, we fought against it. And it made everyone hate one another."

"When Helen arrived," said Izzy, "she threw the gray men out and brought Maple back together. Before the goblins had a chance to come down from the mountains and make peace, the gray men showed up with a stolen dragon egg. I presume that became you, Leo?"

"The one and only," said Leo proudly.

"They enslaved the goblins through trickery and deceit," continued Izzy, "and raised both the goblins and you, Leo, to hate everything about Maple. It was all part of their plan to take back the throne."

"Well, we aren't going to let that happen," said Michael.

"You knew," pushed Eduardo, stepping closer to Leo. "Despite all you've done, a part of you knew it wasn't right. That's why you left me behind at the castle. This scroll is the proof you've always secretly wanted."

The dragon was quiet for a moment. He was thinking.

It felt good to think.

It felt good to know that the tiny little part of him was right to doubt the gray men.

It felt good to be free of hate.

He looked at the gray men coldly. Then he opened his wide mouth and growled. Sparks flew from his throat.

The gray men scurried to try and hide behind each other. They were scared. But the dragon closed his mouth and sniffed.

"You don't have to fear me," said Leo. "I'm not going to eat you. You'd probably taste bad anyway. I prefer my food to be a little more colorful."

Johannah gulped, her colorful, rainbow mane shivering.

"He doesn't mean you," whispered Max soothingly.

"No, gray men," continued Leo, "your power is gone here. If you can't find a way to get along with everyone here, you'll have to go find another world to twist and corrupt."

The gray men sighed in relief and slumped to the ground.

The dragon turned to the goblins. "I've treated you so poorly, my friends. The gray men may have guided my hand, but I did nothing to stop them, so I must accept responsibility. An apology does little to correct the evils I've done, but I hope it's a start down the path to forgiveness. I'm sorry."

The goblins were still wary, and still hurt, but they accepted the dragon's apology. They were willing to work through the years ahead to help heal the damage that had been done.

To the Queen, the dragon said, "I'm sorry about all of this. Thank you for showing me a better way."

The Queen shook her head. "I didn't do a thing. Thank my brave friends who have risked so much to come to you in peace. They truly are amazing students to have learned my lessons so very, very well."

The Heroes of Maple crowded around their Queen and hugged her tightly. It was good to have her back.

*   *   *

As time went by, peace once again settled over the realm of Maple. Libraries were repaired. Schools, too. Scientists returned to their labs and began to uncover the secrets of the universe. Engineers built elaborate machines and artists created things amazing and wondrous. People learned how to get along, to work together, to work towards being peacemakers instead of troublemakers.

After a time, the gray men retreated into the shadows and eventually vanished. Everyone was happy. And all was well.

That is, until . . .

ABOUT THE AUTHOR

Jeff Landry is a proud Montessori dad, a science enthusiast and a part-time writer. He eagerly enlisted the aid of his daughter's lower elementary class (the Hill View Montessori Maple Room) to help create many of the characters and story points in this book.

He lives in Massachusetts with his wife, Nikki, and his children, Violet and Orion.

www.thewritelandry.com